APR 13 1994

The
Shoemaker's
Tale

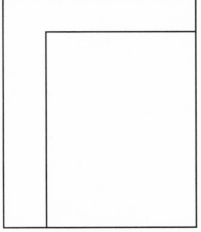

MARK ARI

ZEPHYR PRESS ～ BOSTON

Cover painting, "Sun and Moon" by Paul Klee,
is reproduced from a private collection,
courtesy of Bridgeman Art Library, London/Superstock.

Editor: Leora Zeitlin
Production & design: Ed Hogan,
with thanks to Barbara Miller

*Publication of this book was supported by a grant from the
Massachusetts Cultural Council, a State Agency.*

ISBN 0-939010-39-9 (PBK)
ISBN 0-939010-38-0 (CL)
Library of Congress Catalogue Card No. 93-60853

ZEPHYR PRESS
13 Robinson Street
Somerville, Massachusetts 02145, U.S.A.

*For my mother and father,
and for Janice.*

*My heartfelt thanks to Neil Schaeffer and
Susan Fromberg Schaeffer for their generosity and
encouragement, as well as to Patrick Bourgin* pour
son amitie, *and to Herbert A. Perluck
for teaching me how to read.*

∿

"In whatever world a man is, it is as if the worlds were spread before him."

— Israel Baal Shem Tov (The Besht), 1700–1760

1 🐚

ONE REMARKABLY CLEAR, SPRING MORNING with bright sunshine and warm breezes that blew so gently that even the dust on Warsaw's rooftops remained undisturbed, Meir's parents were slain by a gang of peasant ruffians. Meir was four years old and this particularly cruel Easter pogrom was his first. He and his sister, Yetta, survived by hiding behind the kitchen stove. Yetta had to keep her hand over Meir's mouth to stop him from crying out, and the boy would never forget the dense, suffocating smell of grease.

After the incident, the children's uncle, Mottle the shoemaker, wanted to take them in but his wife opposed the idea.

"Children have too many demons," she insisted. "They are riddled with them. They run in rivers from their noses and found villages in their soiled underwear. Wherever there are children, do you know what you find? Demons by the buckets!"

Mottle, a short man who was almost perfectly round, was no match for his belligerent spouse,

Flanka. There was no arguing with her. Flanka always felt that she had knowledge of things that others could not or would not grasp. Their ignorance drove her to fits of frustration and anger, and she was especially mad on the subject of demons. She claimed that they were everywhere at all times, looking to enter an unguarded person's body through any of its openings. Everyone had them, worst of all children, and everyone was open to attack. Able to travel on skin, in bodily fluids, even a person's breath, they lurked in throats and bellies, waiting for appropriate opportunities. A cough was cause for alarm. A sneeze was an act of war.

Flanka never went about but with a kerchief tied around her neck and covering her mouth. She never touched human flesh without at least one piece of cloth serving as a shield unless she had to. For lovemaking, she cut little holes in the sheets. Mottle had terrible trouble finding them in the pitch blackness that she insisted upon. When he did find one and insert himself, things never felt quite right.

"Your womb feels like a fist," he sometimes remarked.

She would hush him and speed him along. Then, when Mottle was finished, she would go to the washbasin and scrub her hands with soap and a hard brush for a good long time.

Having no children of his own, Mottle wept when Flanka said that Yetta and Meir could not be allowed to move in and beseeched her to reconsider.

"We'll get sick and die," insisted Flanka. "Do you want us to get sick and die? Then the children will be no better off and we'll be dead!"

Uncle Mottle did not want to get sick and die. So Yetta, at age twelve, found herself on her own with little Meir to care for. She began by doing housework for the neighbors, but jobs were short and hard to find. There was some charity from the synagogue and a few coins that her uncle slipped her behind Aunt Flanka's back, hardly enough to provide more than groats, potato soup, and the barest tatters for clothes.

Though Yetta was willing to do anything, no one seemed to want to hire her. Most people had barely enough money for themselves and the wealthier families, those of the butcher, the undertaker, and the moneylender, preferred to hire non-Jews to do what little work they gave out. Gentile servants were cause for boasting among the wives. Yetta, standing at their doors in patched clothes, was more of an embarrassment.

It wasn't until she ventured into the gentile districts that Yetta began to earn enough money to get by decently. The neighbors were horrified that she worked in the homes of the goyim. They speculated openly about the lowly tasks that she was given to do and, slitting their eyes, smiled knowingly to one another when they spotted her on the street.

"Look how she walks," one might whisper, "such brazenness!"

"Such a swagger on a little nothing."

"Her ankles! Can you believe she shows her ankles like that?"

Yetta ignored them and continued to go where she could find work. While Meir was still too young to be left alone, she took him with her. He was no trouble at all. A few rocks and sticks, a pile of dirt, and a pot of water kept him busy for hours. Yetta wondered at what could possibly be going through the mind of her little brother as he clacked and built and splashed with such intense concentration.

When Meir was seven and old enough to help out by doing the housework, she began to leave him at home. Suspicions that the other Jews of Warsaw harbored about Yetta's behavior turned to indignation at the first sightings of her unaccompanied comings and goings in the foreign neighborhoods. Few people would have anything to do with the children at all. Only Uncle Mottle visited, occasionally bringing gifts; a new pair of shoes for the boy, a ribbon for Yetta, who had grown into a young beauty, to tie around her long, extravagantly red hair.

Aunt Flanka was having visions. An old man with an unkempt beard and earlocks that hung almost to the ground appeared to her in her dreams.

"Boil!" the apparition commanded and Flanka did. She boiled everything: meat, clothes, pans, blankets, rags. But when she started boiling the bread and serving it to her husband as a plate of soggy, steaming glop, Mottle threw up his hands.

"Potatoes, I understand potatoes. And meat I can live with. But bread?"

"It's to drive out the demons."

"If you have to, couldn't you boil the flour first and then dry it out to bake with?"

"That's how they trick you. The filthy devils move out and move back in before you know it."

Shoes, hats, books; nothing escaped her. One day Mottle came home sniffling and Flanka got right to work heating large pots of water.

"Get in the tub," she said.

"What?" coughed Mottle.

"Hold your mouth and get in the tub."

"I'll boil alive!"

"It won't hurt you. In and out very quickly, just to scare off the demons."

Flanka stopped as she was filling the basin with hot water, looked at it, put down her pot, pulled the basin outside, lit a fire under it, and finished pouring the water. Mottle stood and watched her, shaking his head, wringing his shirt in his hands.

"I'm not getting in there," he said, but she wasn't listening.

"Ok, now," said Flanka when the water was bubbling well.

"No."

"Don't argue! I'm your wife! In and out, like I said, very quickly and it's done."

"No!"

"Don't you want to be cured?"

"No!"

"They've taken over your mind!" she screamed, lunging at him, trying to drag him over to the tub by his collar.

"No, no, no!" went Mottle, coughing and sniffling as Flanka pulled, pinched, and slapped, all the while averting her face to avoid the demons that were attacking her. She almost had him in the tub when Mottle let go of a loud sneeze. Flanka, releasing him in panic, fell backward with a splash.

At the funeral, Mottle told Yetta that it was all right for her and Meir to move in with him now, if they wanted to.

"There's no need for that anymore, Uncle," said Yetta. "We're doing fine on our own."

Mottle lowered his eyes.

"But," continued Yetta, "Meir will be thirteen in a few years. If you could take him then and teach him shoemaking..."

"I know I haven't been the best uncle..."

"You'll take him?"

Mottle, putting his hand to Yetta's face, pressed his lips together and nodded.

The following years passed quickly. Yetta continued to work for the gentiles despite her bad reputation and the fights that Meir got into defending her name. When Meir was thirteen, Yetta scandalized the Jewish quarter by running away with Stasu Glemp, the son of Wizlo Glemp, a magistrate. The gentiles were equally offended and several Jewish homes were burned to the ground. The local government proclaimed Yetta a witch and sentenced her to death in absentia.

Uncle Mottle was as good as his word and brought Meir to live with him. Although the boy brooded over the loss of his sister, the devoted uncle, with patience and understanding, strengthened the bond of love between Meir and himself. Taking comfort in each other's company, they became like father and son and life went on with little occasion for worry.

From the time that his uncle first began teaching him the shoemaker's trade, Meir thought of little else beside shoes. Mottle watched the concentration of the boy with amazement and laughed at Meir's endless attempts to improve the tools of the craft. He laughed even harder with each of his nephew's successes: a curved, adjustable scissor that cut soles to size in a single snip, a rotating heel to help insure even wear, an oil that made the coarsest leather as soft as a rose petal after a single application.

Uncle Mottle was so pleased with Meir's progress that he built the boy a little shoemaker's cart and gave him a set of tools of his own.

"Maybe now I won't have to work so hard," the uncle teased.

"I don't remember you ever working *so* hard," returned Meir, smiling, chest puffed out as he weighed each of the new tools in his hands in turn.

It wasn't long before Meir, harnessed between two poles, was pulling his cart, clopping and squeaking, through Warsaw's streets. At first, people were hesitant to trust their shoes to so young a shoemaker. He had to run all about, ringing his bell and announcing the cheapest prices in town, in his search for customers. Eventually, some of the more adventurous folk took a chance on the boy. Once they did, they never went to anyone else.

Uncle Mottle got dizzy simply observing his nephew, who was up and out each morning at sunrise and not home again until the sun was long gone. Some of Mottle's own patrons now preferred that Meir work on their shoes. "You should be very proud of him," they would say and the uncle would fold his arms, wink at them, and chuckle to himself. He was proud.

Working hard and happily, Meir was soon able to take on the better part of the business himself, leaving Mottle the time to exercise his good humor in idle chatter with friends and to indulge his copious appetite with loaf after loaf of black bread dripping with chicken fat, vats of boiled potatoes swimming in cream, armfuls of sour pickles, cooked cabbages, and fat herrings. People came from all around to have their shoes mended or to buy new ones from Meir. For two years things could not have been better.

However, as the day of his fifteenth birthday approached, Meir began to have difficulty keeping his mind on his work. Instead he might find himself spending an hour following the slow progress of a wisp of cloud on a fair day. Once, he spent an entire afternoon in early autumn staring at the leaves of trees, hoping to catch one as it turned color. The skinny, scraggly-bearded youth labored just enough to makes ends meet, and that with little heart. He preferred to be left to himself and his thoughts, finding a secluded corner to sit in or strolling absent-mindedly through the streets, eyes fixed on nothing, deaf to the calls of friends.

Not much for studying Torah, the young shoe-maker left the city and wandered on its outskirts when he wanted to feel close to God. He had heard of a great teacher, Israel Baal Shem Tov, who taught that one loved God by loving all creation. That was an easy thing for Meir to do on summer walks filled with the fragrance of cream-colored linden blossoms on heart-shaped leaves, the sweet smell of the poplar's large yellow buds as they clung to drooping catkins.

"I bet he knows important things that people can do," thought Meir of the Baal Shem Tov. "But what use is it to me? You'd have to be pretty lucky just to have a chance at finding a man like that. I'll probably be stuck in Warsaw, shoemaking, until I'm dead."

The weeping willow was Meir's favorite tree. It seemed to have a Jewish soul. Its narrow buds, with their cap-like coverings, held close to thin twigs as if for safety. Though its bark was bitter to the taste, the wood beneath it was light and soft; though its shape was the shape of sorrow, it was a haven for countless swallows with their joyful, trilling descant. In the shade of the willow, Meir would lie down. There, awake or asleep, he would dream for hours on end.

Sometimes, while Meir was out dozing in the woods of Praga forest, Mottle's house would be besieged by the boy's disgruntled customers. Late at night, banging on the doors, tapping at the windows, they would demand to know when their shoes would be ready.

"Soon," Mottle would tell them through the keyhole. "He's getting to it," he would moan with his nose against the glass. "Soon. Soon! SOON!" he would holler into the air.

Meir had to rely on a bevy of disguises to slip by the crowd and back into his home. With false mustaches, dough noses, various shoe polishes and flour to alter his complexion and hair, the boy made surprise appearances that nearly scared the uncle out of his skin several times.

"It's only me," Meir would say and wink, walking over to the workbench, more often just to sit than to do anything.

Mottle wondered if Meir's dreaming might be a sort of madness inflicted by God because of the sins of the sister, or the gentiles, or somebody. But he wasn't sure whose sins the boy might be responsible for. He wasn't even sure about what exactly counted as a sin. All that he knew was that somebody must have sinned. Somebody always does. *Everybody* does, and God had a way of inflicting punishment on somebody for the sins that everybody was always committing. It couldn't be avoided.

Figuring that God must have stuck a dybbuk, some mean, little demon, inside the boy to cause him his present troubles, the uncle set about finding a cure. All types of amulets and talismans began to show up in Meir's room. Mottle, not wanting to aggravate his nephew's condition with worry, masked his intentions behind a pretense of a sudden obsession with ornamentation.

"Very lovely," Meir would say weakly when he found some new clump of hair with chicken bones and feathers sticking out of it suspended above his bed.

"Thank you, my boy," Mottle would reply, always sure that this would be the charm to work the remedy. It never was.

When the fellow whom he bought his amulets from told Mottle that he had a brother who was an exorcist and who had been successful in similar cases, the hopeful uncle went right out to see the man. This exorcist turned out to be a short fellow with a high-pitched, drawn out way of speaking and a disconcerting habit of looking more at the elder shoemaker's pocket than at his eyes as he talked. He also had a large hump on his back that he kept scratching and Mottle didn't like being around hunchbacks. Flanka once said that such a hump was caused by a demon grown overfat from feeding on a human soul. But when the man promised to rouse the dybbuk from its nesting place at the root of Meir's heart, the uncle forgot all and was beside himself with joy.

By way of explaining the presence of a stranger in the house, Mottle introduced the exorcist to Meir as Cousin Beryl from Polnoye. The boy greeted the fellow cordially and showed him to where he would be sleeping.

"I didn't know that we had relations in Polnoye," said Meir when he and his uncle were alone together.

"Sure," replied Mottle, "it's simple; your mother had a brother whose wife had a sister who married a man with three children by a previous marriage, and one of these children, a boy, married a girl whose aunt on her father's side lived in Lvov and was married to a haberdasher who came from Polnoye and happened to be the second cousin of the very Beryl that you see here today."

"And that makes us related?"

"That's right. He's your third cousin-in-law twice removed or something. From me, it's a little more distant. You know, if you don't pay attention to his features, you might notice a resemblance to yourself. Must be something behind the eyes."

"He seems a little odd to me."

"Odd?"

"He has long hair growing on his ears, the outside part..."

"A sign of intelligence. Everyone knows that."

"How about his trunk then? It's covered with grey fur. I've never seen anything like it, or smelled anything like the stink that comes out of it. What do you think he has in there, dead animals?"

"You have to be more tolerant. The man is traveling. He's a bachelor. There's no one to do his laundry."

"I don't like the way he looks at me."

"That's love, family love. Blood's a thick thing, thicker than looks or smells. A little time and you'll get used to each other."

Meir acquiesced and decided to do his best to make his new-found cousin feel as welcome as possible.

Over the following days and weeks, the young shoemaker ignored the foul stench and green smoke that filled the house from Beryl's constant burning of powders. He pretended not to notice the unintelligible chants, the clacking of the dried bones of small animals that the cousin twirled in a clay pot, and the rattles that the fellow shook every time Meir walked into a room. Still, when Meir awoke one night to find this relative strangling a chicken over him with one hand, making strange signs with the other, licking his eyes and spitting into the air, he lost patience and demanded to know when Cousin Beryl would be leaving.

With the failure of the exorcist, Mottle was at his wit's end. His house had become a regular stop for every herbalist, witch, quack, holy man, and charm salesman in the district. He had to hit a few of them with a stick before they stopped coming. Watching the dust build on his nephew's unused cart and the boy's eyes drift further and further away into their dreamy states, he grew ill with worry. Slumped and heavy-footed, Uncle Mottle paced back and forth, kneading his hands and praying, even forgetting to eat.

"Uncle, what's wrong with you?" asked Meir, noticing the change in Mottle. "You don't look well. Why don't you eat something?"

"Me? What's wrong with me? I should eat at a time like this?"

"No eating, no laughing, no joking anymore. What is it?"

"What should I laugh about? I should make jokes when you're suffering?" Mottle raised his eyes to heaven. "He wants me to joke while he suffers."

"Suffering? I'm not suffering."

"Oh Lord," Mottle called, lifting up his hands, "see how he tries to protect me. A boy with such a heart shouldn't be so troubled."

"But I'm *not* troubled."

"See how disturbed he is. He doesn't know when he's suffering."

Sweat began to trickle down Mottle's face. Meir saw that his uncle was on the verge of tears and felt that his own heart would break as well.

"Maybe we should go to the rabbi," ventured the nephew.

"The rabbi?"

"Maybe he..."

"Of course! Why didn't I think of that! The rabbi!"

"Rabbis read a lot. They're supposed to know..."

"Of course! The lovely rabbi! What good thinking! Our magnificent Rabbi Zaydle!"

Walking together, the two caressed and comforted each other down the hard-packed dirt streets, along the white and grey stone buildings and the market stalls bearing eggs, cucumbers, potatoes, and onions. Amidst the noises of haggling Jews and gentiles, floated the scents of freshly baked knishes and braided challah breads. Small boys ran in and out of the crowds, around the slow moving carts, scaring the horses, drawing the curses of broad-shouldered peasants, as the fringes of their undershirts trailed after them and the yarmulkes pinned to their scalps bobbed up and down.

"Look," said Meir, pointing to a water carrier who hobbled down the road, bent under the weight of a yoke laden with two large buckets of water. "That man is soaked with sweat. His face is blistered from the sun. For what? Why should anyone have to work that hard? What do you have to fret about, Uncle, compared to him?"

"The boy is deranged," thought Mottle. "He turns everything around in his head."

Then Mottle pointed to a cross-street ahead where fifty or more cows with their calves were being driven by the shouts and prods of the driver.

"See," said Mottle, "those are confused animals. Their eyes are wide as plates. They don't know what's happening, but something in their hides tells them it's no good. The prod tells them to keep moving anyway. Think of how lucky you are that no one tries to boss you around like that. You can walk in any direction and who cares? For them, no matter what they do, they'll be butchered."

Meir felt queasy. He had so little stomach for slaughter that the thought of it made his legs go weak. Seeing his nephew almost swoon, Mottle feared the worst and, reinforcing his grip, wept like a child.

Rabbi Zaydle sat in his study, his long nose in an open book, moving from side to side. His eyes were nearly invisible behind the high cheekbones that stuck out slightly from his face. When his wife led Mottle and Meir into the room, he didn't lift his head but simply raised a hand, palm out, its crooked fingers held together and tapering upward. Both shoemakers read a decree of silence in the gesture and obeyed.

Although Mottle's gaze was fixed on Zaydle's hand, Meir allowed his own eyes to wander the room. There were chairs of yellow satin and a great, copper candelabra that hung from the ceiling. Old books with tattered bindings filled row after row of oak shelves or were piled in precariously balanced columns about the floor. Cracked, yellow scrolls lay partly unrolled on the table, chairs, and mantelpiece. Light shot through the shuttered windows in beams thick with dust.

"So?" asked the rabbi.

"Rabbi," began Mottle quickly, "my boy here is distressed. His thoughts wander. He leaves his work to walk in a trance or to sit staring at nothing. I ask you, what is it when someone spends more time with trees than he does with people and comes home with a different face every night? He's got a problem, am I right? A sickness! Even as we were coming here, he nearly collapsed in the street. Is that..."

"It's my uncle, Rabbi," Meir cut in. "He's not himself! If you don't believe me, just look at him. A man with a shape like that doesn't forget to eat unless something is very, very wrong. You should see the strange people he's been bringing home and the way he's been decorating the house!"

Before either shoemaker could get another word in, Rabbi Zaydle put his hand back up and they both hushed. Stroking his beard, Zaydle placed a finger along the side of his forehead and looked from Meir to Mottle and back again. His lip quivered. Then he resumed his reading. Uncle Mottle and Meir exchanged glances.

"Marriage," said the rabbi at last.

"Marriage!" barked Zaydle, jumping out of his seat and sticking a finger into Meir's face. "This boy wants a wife, must have one. That'll fix his dreaming. A wife with a good-sized brick in her hands and no more of this nonsense."

"B-but ah...," began Meir.

"Enough!" the rabbi commanded. "Don't you want your father to be happy?"

"Uncle," Meir corrected.

"Do you want him to waste away with worrying about you?"

"No, but..."

"A wife will give you stability and responsibility. Do you have anything against stability and responsibility?"

"Well, I..."

"She'll give you a reason to work. You bet she will, or else! Or is it that you don't care about your father?"

"He's my uncle and of course I..."

"Good! Settled! And what a wife I have for you! A gem! A regular treasure on two feet! So she's a little poor, so what? You're an orphan, as you keep reminding me, and no miracle from heaven either. But you have a trade and her name is Rachel and what more do you need? Her parents were killed in the same pogrom as yours; you were made for each other. She's only a few years older than you. Good teeth, strong legs, or at least they will be once you fatten her up a bit. This is a girl who lights up rooms she's not in. That's personality! I should know; she works right here in this house!"

"But..."

"Mama!" called Zaydle. The sound of running feet scraping on floorboards came toward the study and, when the door flew open, in popped the rabbi's wife. "Send Rachel to us. There's going to be a wedding!"

The wife went as quickly as she came. Taking Meir's hand, the rabbi shook it vigorously.

"A lucky boy, a very lucky boy."

2 🦢

IN THE WEEK THAT FOLLOWED THE MAKING of the match, Meir and his bride to be, Rachel, met several times, always in the presence of the rabbi's wife. The young shoemaker had to admit to himself that he liked the girl. He liked her black hair and the purple kerchief that she wrapped it in. He liked her brown, gold-flecked eyes. He liked the pointiness of her nose and the way that she touched her fingertips to her lips while addressing her elderly companion. Although she was a trifle too fair, tending toward bluish when she was tired, and skinny as well, Rachel's bottom was a full one and Meir liked that too.

Sitting across from the shoemaker, Rachel did her best to avoid meeting his eyes with her own. Moments when he studied her, she sent her gaze high into the air and, cupping one hand carefully over the other in her lap, breathed in quick half-breaths that caused a scant but arresting up and down motion of the starched ruffles of her blouse. Meir watched them.

"Like perfect apples," he thought, averting his glance toward the rabbi's wife who sat with her shoulders drooping, head stiff and curiously tilted.

No matter how hard he tried, the young shoemaker could not keep from looking at the ruffles. The struggle made him itchy. And afraid of the impression that too much scratching might make on his intended and her companion, Meir suffered for long periods, shifting in his seat, rubbing his legs together, wiggling his upper lip, before he would do so. When he did scratch, it never helped.

While Uncle Mottle was becoming his old self again, laughing and joking, making wedding plans, stuffing his cheeks with food, Meir brooded. The boy did not want to get married. He liked Rachel and frequently pictured her naked, but he just didn't want to marry her right now; he didn't know why. So, staying entirely away from his work, Meir abandoned himself to solitary walks to think and worry about marriage.

One afternoon, as he was strolling past the house of prayer, Meir spotted Luckshinkopf the fool.

"Ahwooo! Ahwooo!" shouted Luckshinkopf, arms akimbo, springing this way and that like a hare, head rocking from side to side, eyes rolling in their sockets. Wrapped in rags, his feet looked incredibly large as he waved them about in an eccentric jig. Loose threads and tatters wagged from his torn cotton shirt and the short, soiled trousers that he wore belted with an old piece of rope. He looked as though he were about to unravel.

No one knew where Luckshinkopf came from nor, for that matter, what his real name was. He just appeared one day in the market, holding his arms out like wings and, knees bent, back straight, and chin tilted forward, crowing like a rooster. Everyone was in stitches as the fool raced around after women and children and made several awkward attempts to fly; all the while pilfering a few strawberries here, a few blueberries there, a handful of mushrooms, a potato, a cucumber, slyly slipping them into his pockets.

When asked where he came from, Luckshinkopf cackled; when asked what his name was, he crowed. If someone were to ask him where he was going, he would wink conspiratorially, and in answer to the question of whether he intended to stay in Warsaw, he always responded with a firm, indignant "No!" He never altered his answers in the fifteen years since he arrived, except for the cackle and the crow sometimes getting reversed. People, needing a name to refer to him by, decided on "Luckshinkopf" because he really was a noodle-head. It was more of a title than a true name.

While Meir tried to ignore him, Luckshinkopf did a strange, wobbly-legged dance, his face completely serious except for the rolling eyes. The fool's antics were impossible to resist and the shoemaker was forced to smile. Taking the cue, the joker ran over to the young man, stared him right in the eye, and cocked an ear as if listening intently. Meir imitated him. The mingling voices from inside the house of prayer could be heard faintly, dull and monotonous. Luckshinkopf winked at Meir, licked his face, and started hopping around again.

"Ahwooo! Ahwooo!"

Just then a yeshiva boy poked his head out through the window and pointed a stick at the fool. Luckshinkopf hid behind Meir.

"You'd better cut that out!" shouted the student. "Do you know what you're doing?"

"No," the fool replied.

"You're interrupting our studies! Do you want us all to be idiots like you?"

"Hurrah!"

"And you, Meir," continued the student, "don't you know better than to let yourself get lost in one of your fogs with the likes of that rascal? You'll wind up as illiterate as he is."

"Looks like the dopes are out today," said a blustery voice as a young giant with rippling muscles and a chest like a pickle-barrel rounded the corner of the house of study.

Meir knew the fellow. He was Ezer, the butcher's son. This Ezer had the reputation of a bully and a penchant for nasty pranks. His favorite was carrying off other people's horses and either lowering them into a deep well or lifting them atop the synagogue roof, anything that would give the owner headaches, create a stir, or offer Ezer the opportunity to punch an eye or tweak a nose.

"Are these dopes bothering you?" Ezer asked the yeshiva boy. "Want me to box their ears?"

Luckshinkopf, raising one of his bushy, black eyebrows, snorted and began to box with the air.

"All right! All right! I'm a dope! Illiterate!" insisted the fool, punctuating his words with a series of uppercuts, jabs, and left crosses, feigning first to one side, then the other. "So I can't read a sentence! A single word! But I can recite every prayer and psalm, the whole of the sacred books and all of the commentaries at the same time! Can you do that? I can!"

It was so rare an occurrence for the idiot to speak so aggressively that all three of his listeners drew back from him. Suddenly, Luckshinkopf crowed loudly and then stood perfectly still with his feet together. Putting the palms of his hands against each other, he raised them toward his cheek. He remained silent. All the lines of his face smoothed out. To the yeshiva boy, looking on in horror as the color drained from his face, it looked like a case of demonic possession. For Meir, the madman's countenance appeared to take on a character queerly angelic. Ezer just fumed.

"Aleph, Bet, Gimmel, Daleth," chanted Luckshinkopf, continuing through the holy alphabet. Voice trembling, he rocked back and forth on his heels. His chant grew louder and louder, the tremble turning violent. Then the fool collapsed, twitching and rolling, eyes bugged, letters continuing to flow from his mouth.

The yeshiva student cried out. Ezer, who had lifted his foot and was about to kick the stricken clown in the ribs, stopped short as men began to pour out of the house of study to see what all the trouble was about.

"Murder! Murder!" shouted some of the men when they saw the towering figure of the butcher's boy standing over the rapture-stricken Luckshinkopf. Like a single animal, they fell on Ezer and attempted to wrestle him to the ground.

"You're all dopes!" bellowed the brute, elbowing necks and bellies, plugging eyes with his thumbs.

Meanwhile, taking advantage of the confusion, Meir gathered Luckshinkopf into his arms and, stumbling a bit under the weight, carried him away. After they had gone a good distance, the fool lifted his head and planted his teeth in the lobe of his carrier's ear.

"Ouch!" yelled Meir, dropping the lunatic. "It was all a trick!"

"Ahwooo, cock-a-doodle-doo!" The idiot flapped his arms and bounced on his toes.

"Why don't you get out of here? I've got other worries."

"The choir of heaven sings your praises! Cock-a-doodle-doo!"

Shaking his head, Meir sat down on the ground and rested his chin on his knees. Though Luckshinkopf turned cartwheels and somersaults, chittered his best chitterings and gamboled his best gambols, the young man paid him no mind. Finally, the clown gave up, sat down beside Meir, and mimicked the shoemaker's profound concentration. They sat that way for hours.

"Where is the sense in it?" spoke Meir aloud to himself, breaking the quiet. "Getting married, having a house, making shoes for the rest of my life..."

"Well, if you're looking for sense, that must mean you don't have any and what good is sense to the senseless anyway?" said the fool.

Meir looked up, astounded by how the pop-eyed idiot was smirking at him.

"Oh please, you're not going to be one of those

wise fools that people tell about?"

"Well?"

"Well...," began Meir but the silly expression on the clown's face discouraged him from attempting conversation and he turned away. "What's the purpose?"

"Purpose? What do you want one of those for? They're highly overrated. You get a purpose, first thing you know somebody is expecting you to do something about it."

"Do something about what?" replied Meir, despite himself.

"Your purpose."

"What purpose are you talking about? I suppose that if I had some such thing, I'd have to do something about it."

"Like what?"

"Like fulfill it, that's all."

"Fulfill what?"

"My purpose!"

"Ohhhh, your purpose. And what's so important about your purpose. I suppose you think that it's better than mine."

"I never said that."

"Good! Then you can have mine."

"What?"

"You can have it. I give it to you free and clear.

No charge. I've no need for it anyway."

"You can't do that."

"Why not? It's mine, isn't it?"

"Yes, but you can't just..."

"So I give it to you. I'll hardly miss it. What's the matter? It's not good enough? I'll have you know that I have a very fine one."

"It's not the kind of thing you can just take off."

"I should hope not!"

"You get it and you're stuck with it."

"It's hardly worth having then."

"It is, it is, it's a very important thing to have. It must be. And yours is yours and mine is mine."

"No exchanges?"

"Impossible."

"Phooey!"

"Why phooey?"

"You just want to keep yours for yourself. You're stingy and boring."

"I don't even know what mine is!"

"I'm hungry."

"Is it important to know what it is? If a man doesn't know, what's the difference. He can do as he likes and it all comes out the same. Still, my sister used to say that there are two kinds of people in the world and they're both dreamers; one sits on his dreams and the other follows them. The difference is a matter of disposition."

"I'd like a nice piece of fruit. Do you have a piece of fruit? A pear or something?"

"I've always wanted to do something big."

Leaning back on his heels, Meir watched the smoke rise out of the chimneys and drift in the breeze, forming vaporous faces and figures as it dissolved into the dark sky.

"Have you heard the stories they tell of the Baal Shem Tov?" asked the shoemaker.

"The Besht, you mean. That's what we who are his friends call him. We're old pals; more than brothers. I taught him everything he knows."

"They say he can talk to the birds in their own language and read the writing of angels."

"A snap! That's not the half of what he can do. On the Sabbath he cradles the prayers of his followers in his arms, rises through the spheres to the very entrance of heaven, and personally carries them through its gates."

"I've heard that a huge crowd can go to hear him speak and every single individual, all at once, receives the answer to his own secret doubts."

"And very often, a nice piece of honey-cake as well."

"When he looks at you, it's supposed to feel like you're catching fire from the inside."

"Now you might be going a little far."

"They say that he can read the soul of a man with a single glance and see its past and future and its place in the world."

"Oh no! No you don't!" exclaimed the fool, popping up and flapping his arms. "Forget it!"

"What are you talking about?"

"You want to go see him!"

"I never said..."

"Impossible! Absurd! You can't do that! No, sir! Ahwooo! Ahhwooooo!"

"Cut that out! What do you mean?"

Strutting over to Meir, Luckshinkopf pointed a finger directly at the young man's nose.

"What's the path?"

"Huh?"

"Aha! There is no path! Everyone knows it's ladders! And Love! How about it?"

"Love?"

The loon struck Meir a blow across the bridge of his nose that laid the young man out.

"And there you have it," pronounced Luckshinkopf. "So you see the kind of preparation you would need."

Jumping and dancing around Meir, the clown continued his jibes as the shoemaker lunged after him.

"And you want to meet the Besht? You who doesn't even know what love is? Ha! Cock-a-doodle-doo! There's this love and that love, skinny love and fat love. All kinds! All kinds! And not all of a piece, if you get my meaning, you worm, you mud-pie. You want to find a holy man and you can't even catch a fool! The Besht? You? Who are you? A little humility, please! I demand it in the name of God Almighty and his half brother, God Not-So-Mighty! Who said that? Blasphemer! Stone him! Oh, ye of little faith! That's it, you monkey; a little faith and I don't mean believing the fish-seller every time he tells you his carp is fresh! Your nose can tell you that and it won't go anywhere without you besides. And you want to meet the Besht? Cock-a-doodle-doo! Birdbrain! Donkey! Pickle-head! Never! Out of the question!"

"I'll go if I want to!" shouted Meir, falling on his face just as he almost had the elusive clown within his grasp.

"In that case," said Luckshinkopf shrugging his shoulders, helping Meir up, and brushing the dust off the young man's clothes.

"It's just that...," began Meir.

"Shhh," went the fool, finger to his lips, eyes flitting to either side. "Slip me a pear and I'll hardly tell anyone."

Meir, unsure of how he had come about the decision to go off in search of the Besht, tried it out on his uncle. Mottle wept bitterly at the news.

"Don't we have enough holy men around here?" he asked the boy. "You have no idea of the difficulties of such a trip. Poland is rife with cut-throats and murderers. You'll get your head knocked off. And what about poor Rachel? She expects a marriage, would you break her heart? It gets terribly cold sleeping out in the open, especially when you're sleeping alone."

Meir stood quietly, listening to all that his uncle had to say. There was something about allowing himself to be talked out of it that he couldn't tolerate. It was a serious decision, he had made it himself, and he would not be swayed unless his uncle had a better argument than any of these. Mottle didn't and, kind man that he was, eventually gave in, adding his blessing. All that remained was for Meir to take his leave from Rachel.

Rabbi Zaydle, who did not take well to having his plans thwarted, threw a fit, turning purple with rage, beating his chest, tearing at his clothes and at the whiskers on his chin.

"A bargain is a deal! A deal like stone is a match! Stone! A mountain!" protested the rabbi, shaking his fists.

Amidst the rabbi's tirade, Rachel and Meir spoke as softly as they could.

"When are you leaving?" she asked and Meir didn't know what to say. He hadn't thought about that.

"Soon," he said.

"Soon? Tomorrow?"

"Sure, I suppose so. Why not? We can be married when I get back."

Noticing again how truly lovely Rachel's eyes were, Meir forgot what he was talking about as he looked at them. This time, she looked back. The young shoemaker began to feel that marriage to her might not be such a bad thing and was sorry to hear the tone of relief in Rachel's voice as she discussed his departure.

"You won't have any trouble getting by. The rabbi's wife told me what a fine shoemaker you are. She said that you invent things."

"Little things," replied Meir with a wave of his hand.

"And now it's like you're inventing your life. How exciting!"

Meir turned that idea over in his mind a few times. He *was* inventing his life in a way or, if not inventing it, at least re-inventing it. Sure. Things were always changing anyway. If the world could reinvent itself, why shouldn't he? What an intelligent girl this Rachel is, he thought.

"Do you know when you'll be back?" she asked.

When Meir didn't answer, Rachel bent towards him and kissed him on the cheek. Seeing this, the rabbi nearly swallowed his tongue and started gathering stones frantically. Rachel said goodbye to Meir and his eyes watched her a long time after she had walked away. With stones falling around him and whizzing by his head, the shoemaker took off.

The next day, with the words of his uncle, the curses of the rabbi, and a picture of Rachel all tossing in his head, Meir set out from Warsaw on foot with a sack containing some clothes and his shoemaker tools slung over his shoulder. Thinking less and less about those he left behind, Meir let his steps carry him into the countryside. On he walked, shaded by the large poplars, birches, willows, and lindens along the road, happily taking in the waving fields of long grass and enormous stacks of rye put up like round, brown temples with pointed roofs that gleamed in the sunlight. Windmills, trees, and churches broke the flat terrain. Above his head, swallows swooped gracefully back and forth in the air while all about him were just the things to catch his eye; blossoming rose trees, white-leafed shrubbery, flaming pelargonium, and girls in white kerchiefs making hay.

3 🍃

GER, KOTZK, AND THEN LUBLIN; MEIR MADE
many stops along the road as he moved from town to
town following the Vistula, working a little here and
there, taking in everything. There was no hurry. The
Besht wasn't going anywhere so why not enjoy the
sights? He found Lublin impressive at first with its
high, white buildings, broad streets, and myriad narrow alleyways. It was so clean that it seemed to
sparkle.

The Jewish quarter was something else again.
Meir had never seen so many diverse kinds of Jews in
one place; secular and religious, orthodox, enlight-
ened, Frankist, and Hasid. Their mingling begat
excitement in the air. Jews in Russian dress discussed Maimonides and the blessings of emancipa-
tion. Frankists, believers that the Messiah had finally
come in the person of their leader, Jacob Frank,
urged the crowd to hasten redemption by throwing
themselves into sin so that the divine spark might be
wrested from its depths and sin itself sanctified. One
woman, taking the cue, ripped open her dress, ex-

posing immense, pink breasts, and writhed on the ground in frenzy. Old men shielded their eyes and ran, spitting as they went. Hasids sang and twirled as a fiddler played. Peddlers, shopkeepers, hawkers of every stripe drew crowds with seductive promises of unheard of bargains while drunken prophets called down God's fire and cripples and beggar children clutched at the trouser legs and skirts of the shoppers.

The largest crowd huddled around a fishmonger's stand where a long line of customers snaked out into the street. Meir, curious why this man's line should be so long when there were so many other fishmongers whose stands were almost deserted, got in line behind a friendly looking fellow with a thin, red beard.

"Must be quite a bargain he's offering," ventured the shoemaker, and the man turned around, swallowing a mouthful of cucumber that he'd been chewing.

"Are you talking to me?"

"Yes, I said I thought that this fellow must have a real bargain on fish."

"Well, true, his prices are more reasonable than most," laughed the man, "but that's not why we're all waiting here."

"Then why?"

"The monger is a genius. Maybe even a prophet!" The man held up his cucumber for emphasis, took another bite, and offered it to Meir, who declined.

"I don't understand. He sells fish, doesn't he?"

"Yes, but only one to a customer and you're lucky to get it. He usually runs out before the line does. The special thing is that when you buy a fish, you are entitled to ask him a question. A big fish, a big question; a little fish, a little question."

"And then what?"

"And then he answers it, what do you think?"

"So?"

"So I told you he was a seer, didn't I? People live their lives by his answers."

"They take him that seriously?"

"See that fellow over there, the straw of a man who's holding out an old, black hat for alms?"

"The barefoot one?"

"That's him. He once came to the monger complaining about how he hated to look on the world, the filth and corruption of it. He hated to see his children turning into sinners. He said he could see the adultery in his wife's face every time she came in from the market. The people that came into his little haberdashery looked like vultures to him and the glint in his partner's eye spoke to him of thievery. The whole world was an abomination in his eyes. So he bought a nice carp and asked the monger what to do so he wouldn't see all this evil. The monger said,

'Don't look.' The fellow shut his eyes and never opened them again. He lost his business, his wife left him and took the God-forsaken children with her to Chelm. No more worries. That was seven years ago, and he's been a happy beggar ever since."

"Amazing!"

"Of course. But the monger's answers aren't always so straightforward. Sometimes he speaks in riddles. You could break your skull over them trying to crack their meaning. You see all the men walking around with signs that have fish skeletons drawn on them?"

Meir looked around and spotted several such men.

"They are interpreters," continued the man, "or anyway that's what they claim. There are dozens of them. For a fee they will unlock the secrets of some of the monger's most mysterious answers. They do a thriving business."

As the line to the fishmonger's table grew shorter, the man turned from Meir in order to concentrate on formulating his own question. The shoemaker, pondering all that he had heard, resolved to stay and test this prophet himself. Perhaps the monger could tell him what he needed to know. Then he wouldn't need the Besht, could cut his trip short, and get home to marry Rachel. Meir thought about her naked.

When his turn came, Meir found himself peering directly into the black eyes of the monger seated behind the table. A tiny tip of pink tongue licked chapped lips that were framed by a ragged mustache and a frizzy, white beard. The monger's skin was brown, furrowed, and covered with scaly dry patches. A cold chill swam up and down the shoemaker's spine.

"I-I'd like t-to ask...," Meir stammered.

"First a fish!" commanded the monger.

Selecting a medium-sized carp for four kopeks, Meir moved to put the money down on the table. The monger smiled and the hair on the back of Meir's neck bristled as a bony, six-fingered hand closed over his own to take the money.

"Now the question," said the monger as he removed the fish from the pail, banged its head against the table, and began wrapping it.

"Do you really have the answers to all questions?"

It seemed to the shoemaker that a tiny fire flared in the monger's eyes.

"Answers are not difficult. A good question takes thought, sometimes wisdom. A good question reveals its own answer."

Meir waited for more. The monger finished wrapping the fish, folded his hands, and smiled again.

"Well," continued Meir, "does that mean..."

"One fish, one question!" cut in the monger.

"But..."

"One fish, one question!" repeated the monger, slapping Meir in the face with the fish as he gave it to him.

Meir walked away rubbing the side of his face, confused by what had happened, and embarrassed by the laughter of the crowd. Growing angry, he was determined that the fishmonger would not get off so easily. He marched back toward the end of the line, tossing his fish to the ground where it was quickly seized upon by a pack of voracious cats. As he was about to get back on line, Meir met with an assortment of kicks and slaps.

"Cheat!" yelled a man with a big bug-eye.

"One a day," instructed a squirrelish young fellow from behind a pair of enormous bifocals. "Those are the rules."

"And rules are rules!" announced a woman with teeth like a horse. "There are never enough fish to go around as it is!"

Between the heads of the mob around him, Meir caught sight of the monger's persistent smile once again. Setting his teeth, the shoemaker stormed off.

The following morning, Meir showed up early in order to be first on line when the monger arrived. Shopkeepers and peddlers straggled in and set up their wares as the sun rose over the filling streets. Dogs scurried out of the way of passing carts. Children babbled as they trudged off to Hebrew classes, their arms burdened with lesson books.

Meir yawned. He had not slept well. Forced to conserve what little money he possessed, he had spent the night in a barn without the owner's knowledge. Having stealthily made his way in without being noticed, Meir crept into an oxcart where he had hoped to spend a restful night, only to make the painful discovery that the space was already occupied by piles of scythes, sickles, hoes, and rakes. The noise that ensued brought the woman of the house to the barn door, listening carefully as Meir held his breath. When she had satisfied herself, she left, leaving the shoemaker to make a bed for himself *under* the cart. Then, just as he was getting comfortable, the door opened and the farmer's wife cooed invitingly, tossing in a handful of stale bread crumbs, several of which hit Meir in the face.

Now, waiting impatiently for the monger, Meir burned with the events of the day before, the bruises incurred inside the oxcart, and the insult of being mistaken for a pigeon which, somehow, Meir felt the monger was responsible for as well. When the monger arrived, Meir faced him with a bold and challenging look. The monger smiled. Slapping down four kopeks, the shoemaker grabbed a carp from the pail and held it aloft in one hand.

"My question is what is the purpose of a man's life?" Meir's voice trembled with emotion as he spoke and tried to stare down the hook-nosed monger. But the monger merely broadened his smile, showing rows of small, sharp teeth. Grabbing back the fish from Meir's hand, he knocked it out and started wrapping.

"If you mean by purpose something to do, then that is exactly it. Even doing nothing is a form of doing something."

"That's it? That's the answer?"

"One fish, one question."

"Thief! What kind of..."

Meir was cut short by a fish in the face that sent him reeling into the street where he landed on his bottom, cursing at the top of his lungs while half a dozen cats scurried across his lap to procure the abandoned carp. Two interpreters rushed forward and helped him to his feet.

"For two rubles I shall make the words of the seer as plain as your hat size," spoke the first interpreter.

"For one ruble all the secret meanings will jump out of the words and bow before you," offered the second interpreter.

"For fifty kopeks I will show you how to penetrate

obscurity like a bridegroom," bid the first interpreter, helping Meir to his feet and brushing the seat of the shoemaker's pants.

"For twenty-five kopeks I shall blow the shofar of clarity in your ears," returned the second interpreter, combing Meir's beard with his fingers.

Meir, flinging his arms in circles, set them to their heels and kicked at them as they ran. The monger was now busy with other customers and the shoemaker moved closer to listen.

"When is the Messiah coming?" asked a small, Hasidic boy who had just purchased a mammoth sturgeon.

"Now, he's coming now and soon he will arrive," responded the monger, patting the boy's cheek.

"How should I plant my field to best protect it from groundhogs?" asked a stocky, middle-aged peasant with a herring in his hand. "From north to south or from east to west?"

"Plow it in circles," said the monger. "That way the groundhogs will get dizzy and give up. When they poke their heads out of the ground to get their bearings, you can bash them with your shovel."

Standing with his arms folded, the shoemaker scrunched up his nose and shook his head. The monger shot him a glance and Meir sniffed loudly in derision. Letting go of a loud laugh, the monger let a thin gob of spittle stretch nearly to the table before he sucked it up. Disgusted, the shoemaker turned and went his way, vowing to return the next day and kicking at the cats that had gathered around him.

Stiffened from another night beneath the oxcart, Meir returned to the monger's line as promised. Although there had been no further insulting disruptions from the farmer's wife, he had spent the better part of the night dealing with the cats that had taken to following him and clung to him with incredible tenacity. Having failed to rid himself of them, he had lured them, each in turn, by calling gently and dangling an old shoe-sole that he had taken from his belongings and cut into the shape of a fish. When they got close enough, Meir scooped them into a sack. The shoemaker was surprised at the profound gullibility of the animals. However, now he was more tired than ever, waiting on line with the extra burden of a squirming sack on his shoulder and the muffled mewing of the cats in his ears.

This time, when Meir's turn came, the monger didn't even look up at him. The shoemaker tapped his fingers on the table. Ignoring him, the monger fixed complete attention on a fish that he was scaling. Affecting a cool air of his own, Meir perused the several pails of fish slowly, lifted a few of the herrings out of the water, and weighed them in his hands. The sacked cats, catching the scent of herring, wrangled furiously. Meir had trouble holding on to them. Behind him, the crowd grew restless and were soon mumbling threats and curses. An old woman poked him in the back.

"I'll take this one," said Meir suddenly, pointing to a small herring.

"One kopek," said the monger and Meir flipped him the coin.

"How do *I* find *my* purpose in life?" asked the shoemaker, half sneering.

The monger looked hard at Meir, as if to say, "so that's how you value your life; a miserable, one kopek herring." Meir started sweating.

"You mean supposing it is lost which is not very likely," said the monger. "Follow your nose and try not to go cross-eyed about it."

"What?"

"One fish, one question."

"But it doesn't mean anything!"

"One fish..."

"One question!" shouted Meir, letting the sack of cats wriggle out of his hands and lunging for the monger's throat. The monger pushed away from the table and fell backwards in his chair. Meir jumped after him. The table overturned, spilling all the fish, scraped scales, and sluiced innards over them. The crowd closed in, slipping and sliding in all directions at once. The cats, having chewed their way out of the sack, seemed almost to fly as they jumped and pounced, hissing and shrieking amidst the waving arms and shooting legs of the slime-covered clot of entangled humanity. Through the limbs and torsos, the shoemaker crawled to safety, a tip of the monger's mustache held in his teeth.

Once out of harm's way, Meir got back to his feet and spit the bloody hairs out of his mouth. Not too far away a group of interpreters watched the scene with amusement. Among them, Meir spied the same two that he had met the day before and, calling in their direction, ran after them. Seeing him coming, the two grabbed each other's arms and walked briskly in the other direction.

"Wait!" called Meir after them. "Don't go! I've got a job for you!"

The interpreters stopped and looked at each other. One smiled; the other winked. Together they folded their arms, tapped their feet, and waited for Meir.

"I've an answer that I need explained," said the shoemaker, coming upon them.

"Oh, so now he has an answer that he needs explained. What do you think of *that*, my dear Peckele," said the first interpreter to his colleague.

"Piffle, my good Shmeckele," said Peckele. "You can be sure that I wouldn't do it for less than two rubles."

"Two!" exclaimed Shmeckele, the first interpreter. "I wouldn't even listen for less than five!"

"I've only thirty-six kopeks," said Meir weakly.

The two interpreters looked at him, walked away a few steps to confer, and shook hands.

"You *are* in luck," announced Shmeckele. "We have a special today, two interpreters for an extra-doubly, reduced, low price of one; exactly thirty-six kopeks!"

"A wonderful deal!" filled in Peckele, clapping his hands. "A bargain! An undisguised blessing!"

"So, it's a contract," proclaimed Shmeckele as he slapped Meir on the back. "What's the answer that's troubling you?"

"Well," began Meir, "What I asked the monger was..."

"Just the answer," put in Peckele. "A good answer doesn't need a question; it implies one."

"Nicely put, very nicely put," said Shmeckele.

"The monger said that I should follow my nose and not go cross-eyed about it."

"Let me see if I have this right," said Peckele. "Follow your nose and..."

"And try not to go cross-eyed about it," Meir

finished.

"Try not to go cross-eyed about it," repeated Shmeckele.

"Yes, that's it!" cried the hopeful shoemaker.

Peckele, deep in thought, rubbed his chin and nodded his head. Shmeckele buried his face in his hands and rocked back and forth on his heels.

"So?" asked Meir.

"So, the money," replied Shmeckele from between his fingers.

Unhooking his purse, Meir handed over the thirty-six kopeks and waited as the interpreters divided it.

"By your leave, gentlemen, I'll begin," said Peckele, turning toward the shoemaker. "First of all, the word 'follow' means to pursue, to see something and to trace its direction; point your feet at it and go, so to speak. Therefore we mean to travel or voyage; in any case, a journey. Movement is clear which requires a particular path and, if a path is particular, a goal is insinuated. It is implicit, don't you see?"

Meir shook his head slowly.

"But what is the goal?" Peckele continued. "This is not stated either implicitly or explicitly and therefore is unknown, invisible, a secret and a mystery. So we have a mystery to pursue. Why is not given. The way is not given and hence, is also a mystery. But do we have a hint? The fishmonger said, 'Follow your nose.' The secret is in your nose. Let us look to it."

Both interpreters examined Meir's nose carefully.

"It is a long one and, but for a minor bump or two, quite straight," pronounced Shmeckele. "It is always more or less in front of you and hence, *nunc pro tunc*, the following of it requires that you go forward."

"And what does one follow but a road," added an excited Peckele. "The nose therefore is a road and since the secret is in the nose, then it is of necessity in the road, a long and straight one but for a bump or two as my learned colleague has already perceived. Do you see how scientific it all is?"

Meir, raising his finger, prepared to speak but Shmeckele interrupted him.

"Let us now delve into the meaning of the warning not to go cross-eyed about it. What is an eye but that which sees, an apparatus of vision. Vision! Do you understand? I'm not going too fast? I realize that these are difficult metaphysical matters. And what is vision but a sight that enters through the eyes, an apparition, an image of something before you. As we've understood, the nose, which is the road, is before you and the most forward part of it, the part that all the rest of the nose follows, and you as well, is the tip. What happens when a person tries too hard to see the tip of his nose? He goes cross-eyed! Does that help him to see it? Of course not. It is still obscured. Only now he can't go forward because, among other things, being cross-eyed can cause debilitating head-aches and make one dizzy. He must halt. If he halts, in all probability, the nose halts as well. Nothing moves. Nothing leads and nothing follows. Nothing can be achieved under these circumstances and the goal, which we already know is a mystery, is now un-attainable. Therefore, my good fellow, the meaning of the monger's words is clear. Go forward but don't look too hard or think too much about it or you won't get anywhere; or 'follow your nose and don't go cross-eyed about it.'"

"Magnificent! Inspiring!" cheered Peckele, ap-plauding wildly. "I couldn't have said it better my-self! Your finest hour!"

"I could never have done it without you," re-turned Shmeckele.

Without saying a word, Meir sat down on the ground and laid his head in his hands. The interpret-ers looked at him, locked arms, and departed. After a while, an old cat with broken whiskers slid up along-side the shoemaker and rubbed itself against him. Meir held out his open hands to show the cat that he had nothing for it. Sniffing briefly at the extended fingertips, the cat lifted its nose into the air and walked away. Meir, not too proud to learn by example, picked himself up, dusted off his clothes, hoisted his tool sack, pointed his nose south and followed it out of town.

4 🐌

MEIR CAMPED FOR A MONTH NEAR TOMASHOV, at the end of the river. Later on in life he would tell little children that, at this spot, he busied himself making tiny shoes for all the animals of the forest so that they shouldn't scratch and bruise their feet so much. Actually, he spent his time strolling and fishing, dreaming about building great things with his hands: giant bridges that spanned oceans, majestic ships that sailed the most treacherous waters. He hardly thought about the Besht at all. When he did, he would scold himself for not being further along on his journey. But with one thing or another and life being so pleasant at the moment, he kept putting off leaving.

One morning, Meir sat in a clump of rushes overlooking a small, blue pond. He was lonely, thinking about his friends and family in Warsaw as he watched the warm surface of the water where moisture hovered in thin clouds and water flies spun around floating, yellow chalices of lilies. A duck bobbed its head, primmed its tail feathers, and glided away. A soft breeze hissed through the reeds as frogs croaked and fluttering birds sang in the beeches and alder groves. A willow trailed its leaves in the water.

Meir was absent-mindedly following the zig-zagging flight of two blue dragonflies when he was awakened by a low, moaning sound that came from the woods. It sounded like a wounded animal. Seized with terror, he heard a second moan that was louder than the first, lingered longer, and trailed away eerily. Meir squeezed himself into a ball and, when the moan sounded a third time, shoved his hand into his mouth, biting on it to keep from screaming. He thought about making a run for the trees, but he couldn't be sure which direction the moans had come from. Lifting his head up out of the rushes, he scanned the landscape and cocked an ear. All was quiet. Meir began to inch his way into a nearby alder grove for cover. Crawling slowly through the grasses and thorny thickets, from tree to tree, deeper and deeper into the grove, he came upon a clearing. There, seated on an overturned tree trunk, was an immense monster.

The creature looked something like a man except that it was more than twice the size and all brown, black, and red as if it had been sculpted out of earth and clay. With its huge, clenched fists pressed to its head, it took deep, wheezing breaths that opened cracks and fissures around the muscles of its chest out of which crumbs of soil spilled to the ground.

"Who's there?" shouted the creature, peering in Meir's direction through two black, empty holes that served for eyes, its mouth fixed into a grimace with teeth like broken stone protruding from its lips. Then, as if the creature had been trying to contain it, an awesome howl burst from its throat.

Holding on to himself as best he could, Meir pleaded heaven to save him, promising to give up overblown dreams and idiotic journeys, if only God would give him wings to fly away with.

"Who's there!?" growled the creature again as it lifted the overturned tree and pounded it with such force against the ground that Meir could feel the tremors under his feet.

Then, its thick neck twisting from side to side, the monster moved in slow, expanding circles, closing in on the petrified shoemaker. Meir felt the world folding in on him. It was too late to run. If he did, he was sure he would be captured and eaten. If he didn't, the same fate was only a breath away. There was nothing to do but try to reason with the beast. It had spoken. It had a mind. Telling himself that a man ought to have the courage to take risks, especially when there was no other choice, Meir held his breath and stepped into the clearing.

The creature stopped at the sight of him, a low growl sounding at the back of its throat. Meir felt an icy shiver run under his skin and wished that he hadn't been so hasty. Walking toward the shoemaker, the creature snarled and bit at the air as it approached, opening and closing its long, black fingers expectantly.

"Good-bye Uncle, good-bye Yetta, good-bye Rachel...," prayed Meir as sharp claws sunk into his shoulders and lifted him up high. "Don't kill me!"

"Why shouldn't I?" roared the clay man.

Meir was stumped.

"Good-bye ponds and streams and rivers and lakes; good-bye flowers, trees, and grasses; good-bye Meir...," continued the shoemaker, expecting a painful death at any moment.

Digging its nails deeper into Meir's skin and shaking him until his teeth clacked and his eyeballs rattled in his skull, the creature let out one brain-piercing screech after another. Meir almost wanted the final smash against the ground to come so he could be done with it. It never did. Instead, after a while, the monster simply lowered him back down and released him. The jumbled shoemaker tottered into the woods as the creature trudged back to its place on the tree trunk and resumed the moaning which now dissolved into a hoarse weeping. From behind a tree,

Meir looked back at the beast. In sorrow, it no longer looked as frightening as it had before. It seemed more of a man.

"Hello," called the shoemaker and the clay man growled.

Repeating his greeting, the shoemaker tossed a few stones into the monster's vicinity just to see what would happen. There was no response whatsoever. Cautiously, Meir re-entered the clearing and approached the tree trunk.

"Are you crazy?" asked the beast, noticing him.

"I'm afraid that's becoming obvious," said Meir, more to himself than to the beast. "Why didn't you kill me?"

"Maybe I should have!" roared the creature, causing Meir to start shaking again. "That's for me to say, not you! You're not the boss! Go kill yourself!"

"You talk very..."

"Everybody wants you to kill someone when you don't want to. I'm not taking any orders."

"Your accent sounds like my part of the country, around Warsaw. Were you born there?"

"I wasn't born, I was made. The rabbi who was responsible came from there. It's *his* accent."

"Ahhh, so you *do* have family."

"What's it to you?" bellowed the clay man, grabbing Meir by the throat.

"Nothing...I...You were...I mean it seemed...in a bad way."

"So what?"

"Maybe I could help if I wasn't choking."

"You! How?"

"We could talk, maybe have something to eat... something that's already dead."

"Why should I talk to you?"

"It might unburden you."

"Ha!"

"I'd pay attention. Sometimes a good ear..."

"An ear?" laughed the clay man bitterly as he unloosed his grip on the shoemaker. "You want to be my ear?"

"Well..."

"Ha! Why not? I'll tell you about it. It's a lovely story; a fairy tale. The rabbi that made me was called Simon and was a very rich man, the richest in all the village of Pupekle. He had a satin coat for every day of the week and sable hats brought all the way from Crakow." The clay man stopped for a moment, leaning toward the shoemaker until their noses were almost touching and Meir could feel the creature's hot breath on his face. Looking deeply into Meir's eyes, it continued.

"And silk. Do you want to know *how* rich he was? He had so much silk that he was swimming in it: silk shirts, silk stockings, silk trousers, silk tablecloths, silk underclothes, silk lamp shades, silk drapery, silk handkerchiefs, silk napkins, silk covers for his prayer books, silk skullcaps, silk sheets for his goose-feather mattress. It would take a week to list all the things of silk that he had, and fine linens, and Indian tapestries, and all the things of gold and silver like candlesticks and chamber pots and goblets, or the rare treasures such as beautifully inscribed holy books, and Swiss clocks, and mosaics, and stained glass. No one could tell how he came by these things. He never left the village, though many important people came to see him; landowners and generals, even princes!"

Pausing yet again, this time to study Meir's face for the effect of his words, the clay man was pleased by his listener's gaping wonder.

"Where did it come from?" continued the creature. "There was a steady flow of packages and crates that were being shipped to him from all over the world, from places as distant as China, Arabia, and America. You would think that he'd be satisfied, that he might share some of his good fortune with the poor, of which Pupekle had plenty. But he kept it all for himself. He never married for fear that his wife would have daughters and the thought of carving off bits of his wealth for dowries was enough to make him choke. What he did was expand his house. Constantly and from day to day. It was like a living thing the way it grew; a new compartment here, an extension there. Growing, growing, growing.

"The richer he became, the greater was his fear that others might wish to take some of his fortune away from him. He began to fail to show up at Sabbath services, leaving his congregation adrift. Instead, he sat in solitude, devising methods for protecting what was his. He bought vicious dogs and always kept them a trifle hungry. He built a moat around his home that was so wide that it took fifteen minutes to walk across the drawbridge when it was down. Ha! He had to fill it back in because the dogs kept falling into it and drowning."

"Good!" agreed Meir and the creature nodded.

"With books of magic, sorcery, and Kabbalah, he had contrived a library of the most forbidden wisdom and unthinkable deviltry," the clay man went on in a hushed tone, hunching his shoulders as though he expected his words to bring a blow from above. "No one suspected or they would have taken the house down brick by brick and him along with it. Every evening, in a little, candle-lit vestibule, he pored over the faded lettering on the cracked, gossamer-thin pages that left a residue of yellow dust on his fingers.

"All this that I am telling you are the things that I learned or pieced together only later. I was not yet born as I am. I was not an 'I' at all, but a part of the soil on which your feet are placed and the woods and grasses as well. The wind sang through me, rains filled me, all the movements of animal and insect stirred in my heart. My mouth was the songs of birds; my compass, the reaches of the earth."

The demeanor of the creature began to change. Its eyeless eyes, no longer trained on the shoemaker, locked into a blank stare. Raising itself to its feet, the clay man now spoke in a voice troubled by a hint of a quiver as Meir followed its every movement and utterance with relentless concentration.

"And then I had eyes to open. When I did, there was the rabbi, smiling, gazing down his nose through his own two hungry, excited eyes, the long nails of the fingers of both hands tapping feverishly against his teeth. I could feel the cool earth against my back and I tried to let myself melt back into it. It was the books. With their magic, the rabbi had molded me from the moist earth of the river bank, inscribed one of the ineffable divine names on my forehead, and with a blast of his breath in my nostrils I awoke, and was severed forever.

"He commanded me to sit up in a voice that was like a chirp in my ears. I obeyed. He commanded me to speak and my mouth moved. Begging to be of service, I rolled my face toward his feet and licked at his sandals. Biting his knuckles and laughing, he looked me all around. What a laugh it was; a wheezy cackle, a death rattle. I could have smashed him with one hand. I longed to, but I had no power to act against him.

"At first, I was used simply to guard his vast and varied treasures. Endlessly, I moved through the wide halls, criss-crossing corridors, and spiraling catacombs. Preferring to walk in darkness, I felt my way along the geometry of walls, listening to the yowls and whistles of the rare animals and exotic birds that, with their golden cages and bronze chains, adorned the mansion. When I passed them, their bestial cacophony swept through me like a wave.

"My sleeping place was in a great, steaming terrarium amidst gargantuan fauna; greens and purples, dazzling yellows, blood reds. Its air was heavy with water that rose from a bubbling lake, heated by a subterranean furnace and never permitted to cool. Lying there, I prayed for spores to bury themselves in me, for seeds to root so that a jungle might grow and suck me through its thirsty stems into leaf and flower and, through decay, back into the air and earth.

"There were other ways, the rabbi discovered, that I could be useful to him. Into the forest I went, throttling wild beasts. Their unpierced skins and furs proved a lucrative business. Then I was put to work on the expansion of the palace; hauling timber, lifting beams, raising ceilings and columns. Between times, I carried the rabbi on my back, touring him through the house and surrounding lands. My only respite was the few short hours that I spent each night in the terrarium.

"Then the idea came to the rabbi of lending me out, at a fee, to the neighboring villages as protection from official harassment or pogrom. The news spread beyond those villages in every direction. Rumor spoke of a 'New Samson' in Pupekle, come to deliver God's vengeance to those who had so long terrorized and butchered his chosen people. Some said that I was the servant angel of the Messiah and proclaimed the advent of a new age which would see Rabbi Simon enthroned in Jerusalem. The rabbi couldn't have been more pleased. He began to hold court, receiving only wealthy individuals and village representatives who all brought him offerings of tribute. There was talk of a Jewish Crusade that would carry his banner into the holy land and purify it for his arrival while he waited in Pupekle.

"Ah, but the pilgrims began to appear. He hadn't thought of them. Arriving in small groups at first, they camped on his grounds, littering his yards and trampling his gardens. Soon they were a multitude; lepers, cripples, blind men, swarms of wretched and desperate souls surrounding the house and sending up ceaseless cries for pity. What a sight they were!

"In his chambers, the rabbi paced and smoldered. The wails of the masses joined the excited din of his beasts and echoed in the spacious halls, slipping under the doors and through the spaces in the floorboards, humming in the glass of shut windows. He called me.

"'Disperse them!' he shouted. 'Get rid of them! All! Without mercy!'

"With a yowl, I burst upon them like a devil, swinging a young, flaming willow in huge arcs, showering them with sparks, scorching their backs. I flung them like pebbles. They pleaded and I stuffed their mouths. Their necks snapped in my fingers and armloads of ribs cracked in my embrace. I blew them away like smoke as the rabbi watched, smiling with glee, fingers tapping nervously at his teeth. Behind the mansion, barely visible on the line of the horizon, I saw the helmets of approaching soldiers. I knew that they too had heard of the 'Messiah' and had come to test his power.

"The rabbi had also spotted the invading army and was trying to signal me from his window. Shouting with all of his might, his body shook and veins popped out along his neck. Despite his frantic efforts, his voice couldn't penetrate the groans and tortured screams of our victims to reach me. Without the sound of a new command to break the former one, my course could not be altered. So, with a fury that was beyond myself, I hounded the last remnants of the miserable vagrants further and further into the countryside, glancing back occasionally to thrill at the sight of the wildly gesticulating rabbi."

Going silent, the clay man stood with a rapturous smile on its face, nodding its head. Meir sat and stared, dazed by the creature's tale and the throbbing of his own heart. When the creature failed to rouse itself from its trance, the shoemaker approached it and touched its hand to see what it felt like. The monster jolted and turned on the man with a venomous hiss that sent Meir into a dead faint.

After a few minutes, Meir came back to himself and found the creature kneeling over him.

"I thought you were dead," said the beast.

"Me too," replied Meir, noticing the inscription on the creature's brow. He wondered what would happen if the word were to be erased.

Setting the shoemaker back on the tree trunk, the monster stretched its limbs hard and wide.

"Ha! You should have seen that rabbi run!" said the clay man. "Like a squirrel!"

"I thought that you said that you had gone into the forest?"

"I did. But when all the pilgrims were finished, I doubled back. I had an idea of what was going on and I wanted to see the rabbi squirm. Figuring that I was safe as long as he didn't command me to do anything, I was careful to be as quiet as a stone and to stay out of his sight. I crept back into the house. It was just as I had suspected. He was crazy with fear, running up and down stairs, in and out of doors. It never occurred to him to run out of the house and leave his treasures. No, he just kept peeking out of the windows to make sure that the soldiers were really still coming and every time he did, he got frightened all over again. It was beautiful to see. I followed him about, making sure to unloose the chains and unhinge the cage doors of all of his animals. In no time, the passageways and corridors were swarming with life. Everywhere that the rabbi turned was a new and more unexpected danger. His screams alternated with a dog-like whimpering. And then the soldiers were breaking down the doors!

"Rather than risk being seen by some idiot whose calls might awaken the rabbi to my presence, I retreated to my terrarium. But first, I removed several lighted torches from their sconces and scattered them about. Then, on the warm soil of the terrarium floor, with the rabbi's hysterical weeping mixing in the distance with the thuds of racing boots, the yells of the soldiers, and all the sounds of the animals, I went to sleep and prayed to die.

"The night had passed when my eyes opened and I rose up in the midst of the charred rubble that had been the rabbi's house, covered with soot and warm ash. The walls and towers had fallen in on its web of passages; scattered flames still licked at the broken beams and pieces of collapsed ceiling. Black smoke drifted from the ruins, carrying the aroma of burnt flesh and hair. In the middle of it all, impaled on three long sticks, was the rabbi's naked body, his dead eyes rolled upward and frozen. Hanging from a stick that stuck out of his belly was a sign with the scrawled phrase, 'Gone To Find A Kingdom.' That was the end of the rabbi, but not of me. I've been alone ever since."

The clay man held out his hands for Meir to see.

"All the blood is still here," said the creature, "mixed with the dry mud and clay."

Meir took one of the hands in his own and, as the monster lowered its head, glimpsed again the lettering on its brow. Perhaps simply removing the word would help the creature to end its misery and, by extension, save the life of the next unwary soul who might stumble upon the beast without the protection of a heart as stout as his own. He had the tools to do the job.

"Lift me up," said the shoemaker. "Put me on your shoulders."

The clay man did as he was asked. Meir, running his fingers along the deeply carved letters, lost heart. After all, he *was* only a shoemaker. What good were his skills against such magic? This was one of the names of God; it might be a sin to touch it. Then the creature let out another of its heart-rending moans. Without any more hesitation, the shoemaker, biting his lips, removed a small chisel, a file, and a polishing cloth from his sack and went to work. More and more confident as he progressed, Meir was soon whistling and polishing away the last traces of the rabbi's script.

"In this life, one always gets what he doesn't want and never knows until it's too late," said the monster.

"You know, you and I are a lot alike in our very different ways," said Meir.

Snorting, the clay man began to crumble.

"Wait!" shouted the shoemaker. "Put me down first!"

It was too late. Meir felt a rumble beneath him as cracks formed along the creature's body and split into jagged rifts. Both of its arms broke loose, hitting the ground with muffled thuds and sending up clouds of dust that stung the shoemaker's eyes. The shoulders softened, fell in on each other, and slid away. Meir tumbled amidst large chunks of dry earth, landed on his back, and struck his head against a stone. Slipping into darkness, he thought that he could feel the heart of the earth beating through him.

5 🐚

AWAKENING TO THE CLICKS AND WHIRS OF crickets and cicadas, the unaccustomed comfort of a feather bed, and the greasy smell of cooking in his nostrils, Meir blinked his eyes to get them used to the sunlight that was streaming through an open window. One eye hardly moved at all. That whole side of Meir's face was swollen out of all proportion and ached. White, cotton curtains wafted in a breeze, but the room was warm and the sheer blanket that covered Meir was dampened with sweat.

Through his good eye, he saw a woman standing before a fireplace with her back to him. Bending over and wielding a long stick, she maneuvered the embers beneath two skewered chickens into a flat, even bed as they hissed and flared with dripping fat. Waves of red hair overflowed her shoulders and fell to a point just below her waist where her purple skirt, drawn tight across her hips, clung and revealed shapely lines. Stepping back from the heat, she lifted the skirt's folds to examine the traces of splattered grease.

When she turned toward Meir, he pretended to still be asleep and struggled to keep his breathing steady as her footsteps approached. Seating herself on the edge of the bed, she placed a hand on his brow. Her touch was light, almost a caress. It eased him. Then, feeling a wet cloth being drawn across his face and chest, the cool water hitting his belly and trickling down his sides and around his hips, the young shoemaker realized he was naked. A door opened and Meir heard the heavy clunking of boots.

"Giving him a bath, eh?" said a good-humored male voice. "And in my own home! What should I say?"

"Say anything you like," replied the woman. "*You* found him. His fever was about to burn a hole in the bed."

"I suppose you expect me to believe that he's really been asleep for two days," said the man, taking a closer look at the shoemaker. "He looks hideous."

"You wouldn't look so good either if you took the bang that he did. Besides, I like his skinny body after a bear like you."

"A bear, am I? Maybe the kind of bear to eat you!"

The man let out a roar and grabbed the woman in both arms, growling and biting at her neck and breasts, pinching her bottom with his massive hands while she kicked and choked on her own laughter.

"A bear is what you said," he mumbled into the hollow of her neck.

"A bear? I said a bear? A beast! A devil! Twice a devil! Put me down! Don't you have work to do? Ha-oh! All right! I take it back!"

Softening his grip, the man allowed her to push him away. She eyed him warily and straightened her skirt, betraying her angry pose with a half smile.

"Has he said anything?"

"Nothing but gibberish about monsters and God knows what all. Oh, and something about his nose," she giggled. "Do you think he's crazy?"

"He looks to be a Jew, doesn't he? Anyway, I must be crazier than he is. I brought him home. I should have left him to the wolves for all the work I lost. We'll never get to heaven at this rate. Look at him, sleeping like a rock in our bed."

"It's a big bed," she said, moving toward the man, pressing her belly up against his. "You're missing work anyway."

"I could put him on the floor for now."

"Just be careful not to hurt him."

In one movement, the man's hairy arms slipped around Meir's shoulders and under his knees, scooping him into the air. The shoemaker started and flayed his arms. Escaping the man's grip, he dove behind the bed.

"It's alive!" laughed the man, still holding the blanket that Meir had been wrapped in.

The shoemaker poked his head up, perused his company, and saw the woman's face for the first time.

"Yetta?" he said and the couple looked at each other in surprise. "Yetta! It's me, Meir!"

Taking a step toward the shoemaker, Yetta studied the head that lay with its chin resting on the edge of the mattress. Then she turned to her husband and shook her head. Meir pleaded with her to believe that he was who he was. She remained unconvinced. His bearded face, distorted by the swelling, simply bore no resemblance to the image of her brother she had kept in her memory. Finally, the shoemaker threw up his hands in frustration.

Yetta and her husband, Stasu, conferred in whispers, watching Meir out of the corners of their eyes. Suddenly, Meir pulled a sheet from the bed, wrapped himself in it, and began walking around the room in a hunch-shouldered, knee-bent fashion.

"You should always change your clothes several times a day," he said in a cracking, high-pitched voice as Stasu lifted a shovel that had been leaning against a wall and held it aloft like a club. "Especially your underclothes! It confuses the demons! Men's clothes to women's and back again; that shakes them up!"

"Aunt Flanka!" cried Yetta.

"Yes!" cheered Meir, but his sister regained herself quickly and continued to regard him with suspicion.

"Who was her husband?" she asked.

"Uncle Mottle, who else?"

"What's his living?"

"A shoemaker like me. He taught me. You gave me to him when you ran away."

There was a tone of accusation in Meir's voice that made Yetta flinch. Stasu, alarmed at the pained expression on his wife's face, firmed his grip on the shovel and was about to swing when he was stopped by the crying of a baby that came from a cradle near the fireplace.

"I'm an uncle!" shouted Meir.

Directing the reluctant Stasu to see to the child's needs, Yetta bore down on the shoemaker.

"Who is the ugliest man in Warsaw?" she demanded.

"When you were there it was Eizik, the son of Yekel the barber, with his little pig eyes and nose and a tongue he could clean his ears with. But since then, Nahman the dairyman fell asleep one morning when he should have been milking, and a cow sat on his face."

"What? A cow? How did that happen?"

"How should I know? It was tired."

Yetta had to admit that this fellow was fast with the answers. If he was a sharper, he was good one. Then again, maybe he really was Meir. Placing one hand on the lower part of his face to block out the beard, and the other on its swollen side and forehead, she squeezed to compensate for the swelling. Ignoring the young man's screams, she studied closely the one blinking eye that was visible and the nose that stuck out between her fingers. Meir, unable to breathe because of the smell of grease on her hands, was ready to kick her when she pulled him to her and smothered his cheeks with kisses.

Throughout the following week Yetta nursed her brother with all of the love and attention that she had stored within her. She babied him. Meir was not permitted to take one step out of bed except when nature demanded. At those times, Yetta would make him drape an arm around her shoulders so that she could support him on the way to the outhouse and back. The rest of the time she fluttered about busily, preparing him soups, doing the housework, and talking incessantly. She was so excited by the lucky fate that had delivered her brother to her doorstep that she refused to be bothered by the fact that all the conversation was one-sided. Meir was decidedly cold towards her. Yetta blamed it on the after-effects of the fever.

Stasu had little to do with his reticent brother-in-law. He was rarely in the hut. Rising at sunrise, he would go to inspect the traps that he had lain for various animals whose furs, along with the firewood that he would chop, provided the wares that he took to sell in a nearby village. Every day, before leaving with his goods, Stasu donned a large, loose cowl that hid his face in its shadow.

"My father has big eyes that go everywhere and never sleep," he once explained to the shoemaker.

After sundown, Stasu would return from the village, eat quickly, take up his shovel, and disappear until far into the night. When he was gone, Yetta would give up trying to converse with her brother and start lighting candles. She had candles everywhere; on every piece of furniture, in each corner of the hut, on the window sills, up the walls, and suspended from the ceiling. Lighting each one as if it were a solitary sabbath candle, she bowed her loosely kerchiefed head, brought her cupped hands over the flame and toward her breasts in slow semicircles, and recited a prayer that Meir had never heard before.

O Lord God of hosts
Who confoundeth the Universe,

Cast thine eye toward them that trusteth
* in thy mercy.*
Deliver their souls from death.
Though they fall, let them not be cast down.
To thy righteousness that is like mighty mountains
We commend our lives.

Bending, reaching, standing on chairs, Yetta repeated the ritual until every wick had been lit and the hut was ablaze with a hundred wriggling points of light. Then she'd extinguish them, one by one, until the last flicker was snuffed.

Meir wondered at her behavior, but wouldn't ask her about it. He had made up his mind not to talk to her again until he was dead. She deserved it. She abandoned him. A sister like that shouldn't be spoken to no matter how curious a business she was involved in. So Meir simply watched and listened until, hearing Yetta prepare for sleep, he turned in as well.

Though still not permitted much exercise, Meir was soon spending hours seated at one of the windows. The hut was situated on a narrow promontory high above a great lake, a swell in one of the tributaries that was fed by the waters of the Vistula. Through the window, Meir gazed upon a sky that dropped like a colossal canopy behind the trees on the lake's distant shore. When he sat back and stared straight out, he felt as though the hut was hovering in the air, floating like a heavenly chariot.

Eventually, Yetta could no longer blame Meir's obstinate silence on his injury. It got on her nerves. She made several attempts to draw him out, but failed each time. A stern expression and clamped lips were Meir's only responses to her pleas to him to tell her what possible grudge he could harbor after so long a separation. The quiet was maddening and she waged a war against it, clanging pots as she scrubbed them, beating the rugs with fierce blows, knocking against the table and overturning chairs as she swept. The baby wailed.

At last, no longer able to contain herself, Yetta took up a wooden spoon and threw it at Meir with all of her might, hitting him on the arm. With the spoon had gone her last remaining restraint. Pots, plates, bowls, dirty clothes, candles, shoes, and chairs came down on the shoemaker in a torrent, driving him behind the bed for refuge. The contents of the hut piled up around him and Yetta, having nothing left to throw, pounced on the debris herself. Meir crawled under the bed, out the other side, and ran through the door. Rushing across the front yard, intent on the safety of the forest, he was more than halfway to the fence when the ground gave way beneath him. The shoemaker found himself clinging for his life, staring up out of the mouth of a deep hole.

"Help!" he called.

Yetta knelt beside the opening and looked down.

"Help!" cried Meir again.

"Oh, so now you'll talk to me?"

"Pull me up!"

"Not until you tell me why you're treating me like an enemy."

"Not an enemy; a traitor! A deserter!"

"So that's it."

"You left me with strangers!"

"Uncle Mottle is no..."

"Don't argue fine points; get me out of here! My fingers are breaking!"

"What should I have done? Stayed and been burned for a witch?"

"You didn't have to take up with that Pole!"

"So I left you with an uncle to love you and teach you a trade. What a sinner I am! I'm not entitled to what *I* want. Stasu loved me. He didn't care about Jews or what; he only wanted that I wouldn't have to scrub his father's floors anymore."

"Help! I'm slipping!"

"Who would have accepted us? Why do you think we live in the woods? Do I look like a squirrel?"

"I don't care!"

"Didn't I wait until you were old enough to make

a life of your own?"

"You waited! Please!"

"You have to understand..."

"I understand!"

"Life plays tricks and no one gets the joke. There was Stasu..."

"You had to do it!"

"Can't you find it in your heart to..."

"Forgive! I forgive! As God is my witness, I forgive!"

Yetta took Meir's arm and pulled him out of the hole.

Holding his heart and breathing heavily, Meir put an arm around his sister and kissed her hair.

"Maybe we've both learned something," said Yetta.

"Yeah," thought Meir. "Grudges are for people who don't fall into holes."

They returned to the hut and Yetta, lifting her infant son, began to rock him back to sleep. Taking the opportunity to ask her about her nightly candle-lighting, Meir learned that Yetta expected the ledge that the hut was built upon to collapse. The ceremony was to ensure that God would not forget to reach down and lift them all, hut and grounds included, to heaven before they dropped into the lake. Meir further discovered that Stasu's mysterious night work was aimed at hurrying the process along. The hole Meir had fallen into was one of scores that his brother-in-law had dug in a straight line along where the overhang of the promontory began. In this way, Stasu hoped to weaken the foundation until, simply by shifting the position of a huge boulder that sat on the edge of the land, the whole ledge would break off. Almost certain that he had dug enough holes already for the procedure to work in a pinch, Stasu had set and readied levers at the base of the boulder. Additional holes were more for his peace of mind.

It was all a plan to escape Stasu's father, Wizlo Glemp, who had never accepted the loss of his son to the Jewess. Convinced that Stasu was the victim of the woman's use of satanic magic, Wizlo had sworn to find them and to break the witch's spell by killing her. For years, he and his men had scoured the country, searching and ransacking innocent Jewish homes. Of late, they had taken to combing the woodlands with packs of wolfhounds.

Meir was afraid that fear had driven his relatives mad. Trying to talk some sense into Yetta, he told her that one shouldn't tempt God by taking ascensions into one's own hands. It was bad luck. He begged her to reconsider and she smiled indulgently, explaining that she and Stasu had everything figured out. Either God made the world or he didn't. If he did, then he was responsible. He must know that there was no place in it for them and he would have to do something about it. Stasu's digging was only to help him along. However, if God didn't make the world, that was that. Something still had to be done. Stasu had heard in the village that the elder Glemp and his men had recently been seen in the vicinity. In any case, all this praying and digging had to count for something. God or no God, it would work because it had to.

Giving up on his sister, Meir waited for Stasu to return from the village. He hoped to fare better with the down-to-earth workingman. When Stasu arrived, the shoemaker caught him as he was coming in the door.

"Stasu," said Meir. "Yetta told me about the holes and..."

"Ah, she told you about them."

"Yes, and you must realize that the idea isn't a good one. A hole is only good for getting out of, not..."

"When I finish one and come out at the bottom of our ledge," began the big man, "there I am! Hanging from a rope and floating like a bird. I could almost fly to heaven myself."

Stasu was so lost in his dreams that he couldn't hear Meir pleading with him to be reasonable. Forgetting to eat, the big man took his shovel and walked back out the door.

All the next day, Meir examined the holes and was pleased to discover that there was no imminent danger as far as he could see. To his best judgement, it appeared that Stasu would have to dig hundreds of holes, a lifetime of work, before the plan could succeed. With this in mind, the shoemaker settled in and allowed himself to enjoy the peace and serenity of living in his sister's home, far from the confusion of a town like Warsaw.

Weeks flew by and Meir might have been content to stay there forever had not a scrawny-looking cat showed up one day out of nowhere. It reminded him of the last cat that he had seen in Lublin before he had gone on his way. It even had the same broken whiskers. Taking a piece of fish that he had been eating and placing it before the cat, Meir thought about everything that he had seen and done so far. Wouldn't Rachel be proud to know how he was doing? He was re-inventing his life just as she had said. But to what end? Had he met the Besht? Was he any closer to anything he had dreamed about than he was before? What would Rachel think about that? The cat, finishing its meal, licked its paws and ran off as Meir made up his mind to tell Yetta that he was leaving.

It was a fine, brisk morning when Stasu and Yetta walked Meir to the gate, each wearing the new shoes that he had made for them. Fat, white clouds moved quickly overhead. The trees, having lost all but a few leaves, vanished, reappeared, and dissolved again in the gathering fog. Yetta stumbled, losing both of her shoes, and Stasu caught her in his arms.

"They keep doing that," she said. "Funny, it always seems to happen near the fence."

"I don't know," said Meir, lifting the shoes. "They're the right size. The heel looks strong enough."

"It's just their way of letting Yetta know that she'd better not try to run off and leave me," joked Stasu, swinging his wife in his arms. "The ones I got are terrific! I seem to be able to work longer in them. It's like they walk by themselves."

"And the ones that you made for the baby are priceless," offered Yetta. "What cushioning! Like they're filled with air! He'll love them when he learns to walk."

Meir smiled and they all exchanged embraces. Stasu pointed out the direction that would lead him back to the road that he had been following before he had decided to camp by the river. Sighting his path by placing his nose up against his brother-in-law's finger, the shoemaker nodded and was off.

After half a day of strenuous hiking, Meir stopped and lunched upon a cooked potato that Yetta had packed for him. Suddenly, he heard dogs barking and men calling to each other.

"There it is!" shouted one of the men.

"Where? I don't see it," called another.

"It's up there! Keep looking. It keeps getting lost in the fog!"

"I see it! On the ledge!"

The dogs, trailing after a particular scent, didn't stop to investigate the brush where Meir had just hidden himself. Watching an armed contingent pass in pursuit of the hounds, the shoemaker spied a tall, gaunt figure with hawk-like eyes. It was Glemp, Stasu's father. Without a moment to lose, Meir took off after them, hoping to somehow sound a warning to Yetta and her husband. But Glemp's men were too fast for him. Exhausted, unable to catch his breath, Meir fell to the ground and listened as the barks and yells thinned ahead of him.

Then, hearing a tremendous grinding noise like the splitting of giant stones and a fearsome crash, Meir jumped to his feet. His heart hammered and blood whistled in his ears as he searched through the soupy haze for some sign of the promontory. Images of the broken bodies of his family floating on the quiet lake flitted through his mind until a remarkable vision occurred. There, as high as the clouds and still rising, appearing and disappearing in the grey, shifting folds of mist, was what looked to be a whole side of a mountain.

After shaking his head roughly and rubbing his eyes, Meir looked again, but the vision was gone. He was sure of what he had seen, but he didn't know what to think about it. He had to go to the lake to convince himself of what had happened and was just setting off when he heard voices and footsteps approaching from far off. Glemp and his men were returning. This time, the dogs would have no other pressing business to distract them and discovery would, in all likelihood, mean his death. Pulling in both directions at once, Meir wrenched his feet from their places and began to run back along the path that he had sighted with his nose up against Stasu's finger, back to the road that he had been on.

6 🦃

MEIR WAS HUNGRY. THE FOOD YETTA HAD packed for him barely lasted two days. Since then, he had been eating whatever wild berries and roots he could find and recognize as edible. The autumn was thinning and the approach of winter forced him to wander further and further for fewer and less appetizing victuals. Passing large fields, picked clean of even the memory of harvested crops by ravenous birds, the shoemaker dreamed of the many fine meals that he had shared with his Uncle Mottle.

Here and there, in patches, were diverse varieties of mushrooms. At first, the sight of them made him smile as he remembered how Yetta had once said that mushrooms were like ideas; swallow them without discrimination and you're bound for bellyaches, if you're lucky. Later, however, seeing these earthy tidbits made his stomach growl and his mouth water. Ignorant as he was of the properties of the individual types, the shoemaker decided against tasting any. Instead, he filled his pockets and stuffed his bag, hoping that someone along the road would be able to tell him which of them were good for eating.

There were numerous villages in the area that Meir was crossing, but not one of them had a Jewish community that he was aware of. He avoided them assiduously, never getting any closer than a first sighting of their rooftops on the horizon, walking around them for miles out of his way. Meir knew that the gentiles had difficulties in tolerating Jews without money and he didn't want to test them. They seemed to take Jewish poverty as a personal insult. It was all right with them if Jews were poor in their own areas, but let a Jew take a step out and he'd better be able to pay and pay double or he'd get what was coming to him. And Meir hadn't a kopek since he had emptied his pockets to the interpreters in Lublin.

Uncle Mottle used to tell a story about a Jewish village that existed in this district, completely set off from the surrounding gentile settlements. This village, called "Cloom," was legendary for its charity, especially that of its leader, Rabbi Yeshua, the handwringer. Many an afternoon of stitching and hammering flew quickly by as Mottle entertained his nephew-apprentice with the history of this man and the town he founded.

Born of a Pishke tailor, Rabbi Yeshua had been the type of child who always gave his toys and treats away to other children. His parents didn't worry very much about this tendency in their son until he got older. That's when things got difficult. Every day, after his studies, the boy would disappear for hours, often returning home without money in his pockets, shoes on his feet, and sometimes without a shirt on his back. He claimed that he was always running into people who needed those things more than he did.

"You'll drive us to poverty," charged his father, Reb Dovid.

"Next you'll be giving away your pants. Then where will you be? Do you know how far a man gets in this world without his pants? He doesn't, that's what!"

"The Talmud requires us to give charity," replied Yeshua with sad eyes, gently wringing his hands as was his habit.

"One tenth! The Talmud says one tenth! Anything more is a sin!"

"Look at him," moaned his mother. "All bones. The food in his hand always finds another mouth."

"One tenth! Do you understand one tenth?" continued Reb Dovid.

"But if I take away one tenth of what I have, then the nine tenths remaining become the whole of what I have left and I must give one tenth of that. So it happens again and again and..."

"But you're breaking us!"

Understanding his parents' concerns, Yeshua decided to go out on his own so as not to burden them.

"Always keep the Sabbath," advised Reb Dovid as he helped Yeshua to pack his bags. "Remember, a fool that keeps his mouth shut is counted wise and don't let any woman fiddle with the buttons of your trousers; they're only looking for a short way to your pocket. And try to stop that awful thing you do with your hands, wringing them like that, it doesn't give a good impression."

Bidding his parents farewell, Yeshua began his many, long years of wandering. In no time at all, he looked like any other beggar, tattered and dirty, without a coin in his pocket and not a friend in the world beside the small animals and birds that flocked around him and with whom he shared every crumb that came his way. Moving from town to town, he grew so thin that the flesh of his face and limbs looked as if it were painted on.

Yeshua was troubled by his poverty only in that he had nothing to give to the people whom he met. Agonizing over the dilemma, he wondered why he had been made with so full a heart and no means of expressing it. Then he had the answer. He could share what was in his heart!

So Yeshua travelled far, speaking of the need for all men and women to be as mothers to one another, giving all and begrudging nothing. Everywhere that he went people gathered to hear him; beggars, thieves, drunks, harlots, and sometimes businessmen and rabbis as well. At the end of every sermon, Yeshua would walk among the listeners, taking their hands in his own, rubbing their palms and fingers as if to cleanse a stain, begging them each to follow his own example of goodness. Those that he touched in this manner became his devoted disciples and joined the ranks of his rag-tag entourage. Even the wealthy, once he had gotten to them, would divest themselves of all property and fall in behind him. Oddly, all of Yeshua's followers picked up their teacher's habit of handwringing.

While reciting this story to young Meir, Uncle Mottle would act out the various characters as he spoke; bending his knees, twisting his fingers around each other, making cow-eyes as he told of Yeshua. But when he got to the person of Shemach, a venerable and ancient rabbi who presided over a large congregation in Lithuania, he became more dramatic. His voice turned brazen and his eyes glared. Standing on a stack of books, the older shoemaker raised his fist and shook it, from time to time, for emphasis.

Shemach was a man of renowned learning, pious and hardened to the letter of the law. Large and warrior-like, he towered above other men. Despite his age, his hair never greyed but grew wilder with each passing year. Fiery red, it rolled in thick curls on his head and in a beard that was so long that he usually wore it under his shirt, tucked into the belt of his trousers.

Receiving the first reports of Yeshua and his adherents, Shemach passed them off as the fancies of the superstitious masses. However, the reports persisted and grew more alarming. Yeshua's beggar army was growing at a remarkable rate. Whole communities were going over to him.

"He'll make beggars of us all!" shouted Shemach when he discovered that some of his own agents had been recruited. "With our coffers emptied, the goyim won't forgive us the air we breathe! We'll be destroyed!"

Hastily, Shemach scribbled a letter to the most important rabbi in the world, the Gaon of Vilna, demanding the immediate excommunication of Yeshua and his gang. The Gaon owed Shemach many favors. Whenever he was perplexed by one of the many questions put to him every day by Jews throughout Europe, the Vilna Rabbi would dispatch a special envoy on horseback to carry the conundrum to Rabbi Shemach for consideration. The response that followed affected the way Jews everywhere lived their lives and served their God. Whatever misgivings the Gaon might have had about Shemach's request, he could not refuse.

News of the excommunications spread, causing the Jews of Poland to fear the very mention of Yeshua's name. Groups of men, armed with sticks and rocks, met the ragged rabbi at the entrance to every town and village. Though none of his own handwringing disciples deserted him, the movement came to a standstill. Yeshua, undeterred, proclaimed that Shemach had overstepped his authority by forcing the hand of the Gaon, that power had corrupted the elder rabbi's thinking, causing him to make judgements that weren't his to make and that threatened to weaken the fabric of all Jewish souls. Aiming his army toward Lithuania, Yeshua promised to convert Shemach or to topple him in the effort.

The part of the story where the two rabbis met was both Mottle's and Meir's favorite. Before proceeding, Mottle would creep up close to his nephew and stare right into the boy's eyes. Hushed, almost a whisper, his voice would rise in tremulous tones.

On a clear April afternoon, at the head of a weathered troop of skeletons, Yeshua confronted Shemach on a border pass that led into Lithuania. The old rabbi, having been apprised of "the handwringer's" advance, had come on his own, ready for a fight.

Swollen with anger, his beard flashing in the sunlight as it whipped over his shoulder, Shemach stood with his arms folded and his jaw set. Yeshua stepped forward to meet him, separating himself from his followers, and held out a small piece of black bread.

"Bribery!" accused the elder rabbi, slapping the stale morsel from the offerer's hand.

"An offering," explained Yeshua, head bowed, wringing his hands.

The ancient warrior, drawn and distracted by the serpentine movements of the young man's slender fingers, had to pull his eyes away.

"You lead the people to destruction with your malignant teaching!" charged Shemach.

"And you would chain them with your mind," countered Yeshua, feeling the material of his opponent's sleeve, slyly edging his fingers towards Shemach's hands.

"False prophet!" Shemach bellowed and swatted the handwringer away.

"Jailer!"

"Tempter!"

"There is no king but God!"

Lunging for the ragged figure before him, Shemach took him by the throat while, in return, the gagging Yeshua entwined his own fingers around the elder rabbi's neck and his legs about Shemach's midsection.

According to the tale, the way that Uncle Mottle told it, the brutal combat lasted for six days and only ended when both of the battlers were too exhausted to go on. Shemach had lost every hair of his beard, the strands lifting in the breeze and blowing away like dust as he looked after them. Limping back to Lithuania, he spent the last few years of his life in utter silence, writing questions that he mailed to himself and refused to answer. The handwringer, for his part, had nine of his ten fingers cracked at the knuckles during the fight. A blow to his back had affected his legs, making them numb and lifeless, and he had to be carried from the field by his disciples. Retreating to an area devoid of other Jews, the very region that Meir was presently traversing, Yeshua and his followers founded the village of Cloom where their generosity became so obsessive that no one wore the same shirt, milked the same cow, or lived in the same house for more than a day without giving it away. For lack of anyone who could hold on to a set of tools or a patch of farmland long enough to get anything done, the town did not prosper.

Uncle Mottle, depending on his mood, had a different moral every time that he told the story. When he was feeling that Meir's mind was too busy for the boy's own good, he would intone, "Big brains are like big balls; they tend to get in your way while you're walking and only give you more to defend." Like most of his uncle's morals, this one didn't seem to have much connection to the story for Meir. Yet, there was another that Meir remembered now and that rang in his ears: "Unless you want your nose poked, don't go poking your nose." Though not convinced that this one stood up any better than the first, he liked it. It made him think of home and how much he missed it. He thought about Rachel too, and pictured her naked for as long as he could to keep his mind off of how hungry he was.

In recalling the story, the young shoemaker also remembered that Mottle described Cloom as having been built on a spot that was surrounded by seven hills. He had never believed his uncle's claim that the village actually existed but, with starvation the only alternative, Meir kept a sharp lookout as he walked.

A couple of hills here, a cluster of three or four there, Meir struggled on without a sign of life to be seen anywhere until he happened upon three revelers in fur hats and coats. They were singing boisterously, marching on unsteady legs, passing a wineskin between them. By the style of their shoes, Meir could tell that they were peasants and made a run for it. But not before they spotted him as well. One of them chased after the shoemaker, caught him by the seat of his trousers, wrestled him to the ground and sat on him.

"Look what I got!" yelled the peasant. "Wiktor! Tomcyk! Come see my catch!"

"It seems that you can never get rid of all these Jews," said one of the others who had big, green teeth. "They're like rats the way they turn up."

The third member of the group grabbed Meir's sack, stuck his long, skinny nose into it, and then emptied its contents onto the ground.

"I get the hammer," said the one holding the shoemaker.

"I don't want any trouble," said Meir. "Take whatever you want. I was only looking for the village of Cloom."

"Shut up!" commanded the fellow on top of Meir, digging a knee into the small of the shoemaker's back.

"Look at all these mushrooms!" laughed Greenteeth.

"Did he say he was looking for Cloom?" asked Needle-nose. "Ha! We should help him find it!"

"Any money?" asked Meir's tormentor.

"Not unless Jews use mushrooms for money," answered Greenteeth, bending toward the shoemaker. "Hey Zhid, you like mushrooms? Don't you know that some of these can be nasty?"

When the man with the green teeth tried to shove a handful of the mushrooms into Meir's mouth, the shoemaker struggled and the man on top of him came down hard, knocking the air out of his lungs. Then Greenteeth pulled Meir's jaw open and stuffed it several times. Meir wouldn't swallow. Disgusted, Greenteeth punched him in the face and broke his nose.

"Send him to Cloom and let's get out of here," said Needlenose. "It's too cold for Jew games."

The threesome divided the goods, added a few kicks and blows to Meir's bruises, and stripped him of his clothing. Holding the shoemaker's head up by the hair, Greenteeth pointed it north.

"That's where Cloom is. It's an hour, if you don't freeze first," said Greenteeth, giving Meir's broken nose a twist with his fist.

The young men departed, leaving the shoemaker stretched out on the ground. He wanted to remain as motionless as possible but, afraid that he might fall asleep and freeze to death, Meir forced himself to his feet. Keeping his hands over his genitals and rubbing them to keep warm, he headed in the direction that Greenteeth had indicated. It was hard for him to walk and the wind bit at him like an animal. Wondering whether the peasant had lied to him about the whereabouts of the village, he cursed himself for his whole insane trip. But then, when he had about given up, right in the middle of seven hills as his uncle had said, Meir saw the tiny village. Despite his pain and the numbness of his feet, he doubled his pace.

Upon reaching the village, Meir began to notice that many of its buildings were damaged, some completely razed. There was an unusual silence and, staggering on to the streets, he found them to be blanketed with corpses; men with their throats cut and heads bashed open, women frozen into grotesque and obscene poses, children hacked into fleshy rags. Dogs tore at the dismembered limbs and fought over entrails, dragging them in their teeth. Meir clutched his stomach and spit blood.

"Hello!" shouted a voice, "Hello! Hello!"

"Who's there?" returned Meir. "Who's there?"

"Here, on the house of prayer! On the roof! Don't worry if you can't see me; I'm invisible."

"I see you plainly enough," answered Meir, spying a plump old man in old trousers and a red shirt squatting on a chimney top.

"Oh? Well, I must be visible again. Being invisible takes a lot of concentration. You have to sit perfectly still. You can't even let your insides move and you have to wipe every thought out of your mind. When you do that, you're invisible. I must have lost concentration when I saw you."

"Who are you?"

"My name's Israel. I heal with my hands, tell fortunes, things like that. I'm not a native here, just happened by. You know, a visitor."

"What are you doing on that roof?"

"Waiting for you! You're the Messiah, right?"

"What?"

"The Messiah! You're him, right? I expected something more dazzling."

"I'm no Messiah!"

"An angel?"

"I'm a shoemaker!"

"A ship-maker?"

"A *shoe*maker!"

"A ship-maker. Yes, you look like one of those. You'd better climb up here right away. When the Messiah gets here, we'll be whisked to Jerusalem. This way we won't get banged on anything on the way up."

"What the devil are you talking about?"

"Haven't you been listening? You get distracted pretty easily; I could tell that right off. I'm talking about the end of the world. It's here! Look around you; can't you tell?"

"I'd get off that roof, if I were you. It doesn't look too sturdy."

"Oh?"

Meir was unable to talk anymore. His bruises ached and his skin was turning purple in the cold.

With his head swimming, he stumbled through the doorway of the house of prayer where he found the floor riddled with torn prayer books and at least twenty bodies lumped in a pile. Lifting some of the prayer shawls from around the shoulders of the dead, Meir wrapped himself in them. The building trembled and creaked about him. Spotting a ladder that led up toward the roof, Meir called to the old man. When he didn't answer, Meir began to climb.

As he stepped on to the roof, Meir looked for the old fellow, but the chimney was vacant. From where he stood, the shoemaker viewed the whole town: the mass of mutilated bodies, the rivers and pools of blood frozen on the streets, the few broken, faltering remains of buildings that still stood above the wreckage. Beyond that, standing with the loose, fringed ends of the shawls flapping about him, Meir saw the edges of the forest where it bordered a peasant village. Coming out of the trees were women in white hats. Although he couldn't quite make them out at that distance, he imagined their gaily embroidered dresses and the nearly liquid translucence of their skin. He could almost hear their pleasant chatter and smell the pine scent on their hair as they returned home, arms laden with full baskets of sweet berries and chestnuts.

Hurting with every breath that he took, his arms

and legs as heavy as stone, the shoemaker laid himself down to rest for a while and felt the building pitch in the wind like a ship on a turbulent sea. He decided that he had come too far to meet the Besht. This was the end of the world. Or maybe that was the world on the other side of the forest. He didn't want to think about it. There could be all the worlds that wanted to be, or none at all. Pulling the shawls tight around his shoulders, Meir cupped his broken nose in his hands and slept.

7 🐾

MEIR, STARTLED FROM HIS SLEEP BY A PERSIS-
tent poking at his arm, struggled to free himself from
the prayer shawls that had become entangled about
him during the night.

"Who's there?" he called into the dark.

"It's me, Israel, remember? I guess I'm invisible
again. Sometimes it just happens."

Recognizing the voice of the old man who had
spoken to him from the chimney-top, the shoemaker
reached out until he touched the fellow. He could
just begin to make out the outline of Israel's face.

"Why did you wake me?" grumbled the shoemaker, feeling his bruises. The night air seemed to
lodge ice in all of his joints.

"You're the one who said that the building was
going to fall down," responded Israel. "Besides, there
are men coming. They probably don't realize that it's
the end of the world and are coming back to get
whatever they didn't carry away the first time."

"How do you know that anyone's coming?"

"I have all kinds of powers. Didn't I tell you? And,

anyway, I can see their torches."

Turning, Meir saw dozens of flickering lights approaching the village.

"What about the bodies?" said the shoemaker. "Who's going to bury them?"

"Bury them? What for? They're just going to have to rise again when the Messiah gets here. You'll see, we're all going to Jerusalem. He's just a little late, that's all. We're supposed to fly or roll or something. I hope we fly."

"If you're so sure about it, why are you in such a hurry to get out of here?"

"I'm religious, not an idiot! I don't care where I wait. But if *you* want to be hacked to pieces..."

Before he had finished his sentence, the old man had vanished again, this time through the hole in the roof where the ladder was. Meir, aching all over, gave himself a quick self-examination; fingering his arms and legs, running a hand along his rib cage, testing the movements of all of his extremities. Nothing was broken. Nothing, that is, except his nose, the tip of which was now at a right angle to its base and pointing left. Then, moving slowly and carefully, the shoemaker found his way to the ladder and down into the house of prayer.

By the time that Meir made it to the street, Israel was already waiting for him, urging him on from atop a dilapidated cart drawn by a sickly-looking animal that bore only the slightest resemblance to a horse.

"This animal looks like the plague," complained the shoemaker, climbing aboard. "It can barely walk."

"We don't need it to walk," said Israel, clicking his tongue. The almost-horse took off at a gallop, racing through the streets with a loping gait, the wagon wobbling behind. Meir had to hold on tight as the cart careened and bounced around turns.

After half an hour or so, with danger well behind them, both men relaxed. Meir put on some clothes that the old man had scavenged for him out of the wreckage of Cloom. Israel, attempting to slow the animal to a more casual pace, pulled up on the reins. Snorting, the horse stopped abruptly, stretched its muzzle, fell over on its side and died.

"Guess we'll have to walk," said Israel, getting down after the grumbling shoemaker and then searching the young man's eyes. "Hey, Ship-maker, are you sure you're not him?"

"Who?"

"The Messiah, who else? You're ugly enough. The scriptures say that he's supposed to get beaten up and have a marred visage. You look like you've gotten enough beatings for a cartload of Messiahs, and that nose of yours is about as marred a visage as I've ever seen."

"I'm not him."

"A denial! Perfect! That's just what I'd expect from the Messiah!"

Meir walked away and Israel, grabbing a small bundle from the seat of the cart, trundled after him.

"Come on, don't fool me," the old man went on. "You are, aren't you? Yes? ...And silent too! Just like I pictured you to be! Admit it, you're him!"

"Listen," spoke Meir, bearing down on the old fellow. "I am no Messiah! One look at me should tell you that! If I were, do you think that I would have run from that town? I would have waited for that mob and dropped the sky on them, or opened up the earth and had it swallow them, or called down a half a dozen thunderbolts and fried them like kreplach! Why didn't I do that?"

"Modesty? The Messiah should be..."

"Get it through you skull; I'm a shoemaker! From Warsaw! I was on my way to find the Baal Shem Tov and had some trouble! *Some* trouble? That's all it's been is trouble!"

"The Besht?"

"Yes, world renowned, hocus-pocus, sacred blowhard that he probably is."

"I've heard that some people consider him a very nice fellow."

"That's a laugh! He sets himself up as a big deal

and fools like me go looking for him, leaving everything; friends, family, a fine match. And for what? Look at this nose! I'm done with it!"

"Maybe he doesn't like the fame. Maybe he'd rather be anonymous. Maybe he couldn't help it."

"Maybe-shmaybe, he's cashing in! He holds court like a king, and you don't think he likes it? He's probably as rich as a pharaoh! Armed guards! Concubines!"

"Wait a..."

"Big saint! And most likely no more of a wise man than I'm a Messiah!"

"Stop!" hollered Israel. "He didn't ask you to come looking for him, did he? What did you think you needed him for anyway? Figure things out for yourself."

Meir didn't answer and the two men walked along in silence.

"Where are we going?" grumbled the shoemaker after a while.

"I thought *you* knew. Where were you heading?"

"South, but now I don't care."

"The nearest town is Lvov."

"Fine. Which direction?"

"South," smiled the old man, reaching into his bundle, taking out a handful of mushrooms, and offering some to Meir. "I picked them myself."

"You do know that some of these could be poisonous, don't you?"

"Sure they can, if you don't discriminate. There's one thing that age teaches you and that's how to discriminate between mushrooms."

"Just so long as you're aware," returned Meir, taking a few and munching on them greedily.

"Of course, my eyes aren't what they used to be."

Over the next few days, the traveling companions became fast friends. Meir stopped insulting the Besht and Israel agreed to stop talking about the end of the world, the Messiah, and going to Jerusalem. However, Meir was incapable of breaking the old man of the habit of referring to him as "ship-maker." He simply had to accept it to keep the peace.

During enthusiastic campfire chats, the shoe-maker learned about Israel's long life as a sojourner, performing minor miracles, dispensing herbal elixirs, and laying on hands, in a pinch, if a situation required it. In return, Meir entertained the old man by talking about his family in Warsaw and the adventures that he had encountered along the road. Israel was especially interested in Rachel and nodded briskly whenever her name came up. Sometimes he would ask his young friend about the shapes of various parts of her body and how they moved when she walked.

Meir didn't bother to answer. It wasn't necessary. He could tell by the way that the old fellow would close his eyes, lean his head back, and smile after asking, that Israel could provide whatever answers he needed for himself.

Meir explained to the old man how he had dreamed of doing great things with his hands and how these dreams had been the cause of all of his misfortunes; leading him, as they did, on this miserable journey in the first place. Then, not wanting his new friend to think him too much of a fool, the shoemaker further confided that he had grave doubts about the plan right from the start. Besides, now he was done with it anyway, and all that he wanted to do was to get himself some new tools so that he could earn enough money to make the trek home with as few difficulties as possible.

"So you don't want to see the Besht anymore?" asked the old man. "You've given it up?"

"Completely."

"And what about your big dreams?"

"Gone."

"Dreams don't hurt a person."

"Look at this nose."

"You worry too much. What if this? What if that? You've got to stop thinking. Like I do when I become invisible. Once you do something without a thought in your head, bang! That'll be it! *That's* when people do things!"

"Who wants to do anything? For whom and for what? There's not enough troubles when at any moment someone might come up and cut your throat or tear open your belly and sew a live cat inside?"

"That's not..."

"Finished-finished-finished!" shouted Meir, going red and shaking so hard that he frightened himself as well as old Israel.

They never spoke about the subject again, preferring to keep their talks as lighthearted as possible. Still, Israel couldn't help noticing the bitter expression that began to develop and harden upon Meir's face.

On the afternoon that they came to the town of Lvov, the ground was covered with snow, stretching out smooth and white as milk through the streets and covering the low, sloping roofs. Israel suggested that the first thing to do was for Meir to get some new tools. That way they'd have an immediate means of bringing in some money. Although Meir liked the reasoning, he pulled his empty pockets inside out to illustrate the fatal flaw in the argument. The old man smiled impishly, dipped a hand into his bundle, and extracted a small pouch out of which he removed twelve shining rubles. Meir gaped for a moment and then pounced on his comrade, kissing him over and over again, promising him the finest pair of shoes he had ever worn in his life.

With a vigor inspired by newfound wealth, Meir pulled Israel along into the town, this way and that, in and out of shops, purchasing everything that a shoemaker requires to pursue his profession as well as some new shirts and trousers, a pair of sturdy fur coats, and a couple of fur caps for their heads. Freshly accoutred and cheerful as children on Purim, the men found an inn and set about settling accounts with their long-suffering bellies. Roast chicken, kasha, gefilte fish, double helpings of large, fluffy matzoh balls in steaming soup, plate upon plate of sugary pastries that left their beards flecked with white powder, all flowed down their throats as they munched with relish, emitting occasional, squeaky noises of contentment and uncontainable delight. The poor woman who served them trotted in and out of the kitchen, breathing heavily, her long, fat breasts jumping like animals under her blouse as she delivered new, heaping trays with one hand and swept away the ravages of their appetites with the other.

"These aren't men," thought the woman as she clasped a chair to steady herself. "They're vultures! Demons! They'll be eating the table next, and then no one will be safe."

"More cake!" called Meir, wishing that his Uncle Mottle could see him now, eating like a master.

"More!" echoed Israel, taking pleasure in the good humor of his young friend. It was the first time that he had seen the fellow enjoy himself.

However, a belly is just a belly after all, and not a magic hole into which infinite supplies can be dropped to disappear.

Both men were soon slouched in their seats, sweating profusely, and holding the distended mounds that hung over the unbuttoned tops of their trousers. After a brief rest, during which she took courage from the display of mortality on the part of her patrons, the innkeeper informed them of the bill. The amount that they owed sickened them further. But Meir paid the woman and the two friends laboriously made their way to the door.

With their fortune diminished, finding lodging was no easy matter. They searched for hours until a lanky, narrow-eyed candle-maker offered to let them use a cowshed he had behind his shop.

"Just stay away from my daughter," he cautioned and the companions nodded happily.

Immediately upon settling into their new abode, Meir began work on a pair of shoes for Israel. The old man watched the shoemaker with wonder, marveling at the dexterity of his fingers, the sharpness of his eyes, the sureness of his hand as it made swift, flawless cuts in the leather. Each stitch was as straight as the one that came before; every nail was perfectly spaced and seemed to disappear as it sank into its proper place in the heel or sole.

"You see the way I let you work and don't bother you," said Israel. "If there's one thing that age teaches you, it's to let somebody do his work. That's respect. You don't want people yapping in the ear of the surgeon who's bleeding you, asking for autographs, do you? It's common sense. He could lose concentration. That's how fame kills people and ruins reputations."

"What color would you like?"

"Orange is nice."

"Orange?" Meir repeated, shrugged his shoulders, and proceeded to mix the dyes.

The next day, after a good night's rest, the shoemaker made sure that the shoes were dry and proudly handed them to his friend. Before Meir knew what was happening, the old man had them on and was leaping into the air, clicking his heels.

"They're tremendous!" exclaimed Israel, strolling about the shed. "I'm as light as a feather! A man could walk clear to heaven in shoes like these!"

Meir, putting his tools away, watched and smiled

as his elderly friend continued to parade with surprising vitality.

"You're blessed," Israel went on. "Did you know that? Especially blessed! Any man who can put his spirit into his work is blessed, but you make shoes with a spirit all their own!"

Spinning like a dreydle, old Israel danced through the cowshed door and away, still singing praises to Meir's skill. The shoemaker yawned, and decided to steal a few moments more of sleep before venturing out.

When Meir opened his eyes again, he realized that he had been asleep for hours. The better part of the day was gone and he hadn't done a thing to raise any money. Splashing some water on his face, he took up his tools and sprang out the door. Rather than take the long way around, the shoemaker opted for the shortcut through the candle-maker's shop. As soon as he entered, he saw a woman who was beautiful beyond all imagining.

The woman was Sarah, the candle-maker's daughter. Meir understood her father's injunction against going near her as soon as his eyes fell upon her. Yet, he let them linger. Her hair was black, blacker than Rachel's, so black that it bordered on violet, and her eyes were a green that an ocean could envy. Although her dress, oversized and coarse as it was, was obviously intended to hide her figure, the voluptuousness of her bosom was impossible to conceal. Where the dress was drawn in by a length of rope, a trim waist was daintily evident. Meir was certain that were he to place his hands on both sides of that waist, the fingers of each would be able to meet.

"She's taken!" barked the candle-maker, pulling his daughter through a curtain into a back room. "A match has been set with Lutik the beadle. Remember your promise!"

Nodding dumbly, Meir kept his eyes trained on the curtain. He had to rub his arms and pry his feet loose from the spot where he was standing. When he finally managed to leave, his heart was still pounding.

Outside, things were stirring. Hasids were dancing with more abandon than usual. Children challenged the cheerful, quick-tempoed tunes of the fiddlers with an array of grinding, clicking noisemakers and the squeaky toots of toy horns. Tables were being set in the streets and covered with white, linen cloths. The rushing of people kicked dust into the air.

Directions were being dictated by a man with a small head and round bushes of hair that stuck out of ears that wiggled with excitement. He was Zimmel the tailor and had begun the hubbub by announcing that he had seen the Besht that very morning, obviously paying a surprise visit to the town. The holy man, who had been walking in the market square, had run off when Zimmel called to him, rounding the corner of a building and losing himself in the side-streets. Nevertheless, the tailor had recognized the Besht from having attended one of the Rebbe's gatherings years ago and was certain that he wasn't mistaken.

At first, some of the townspeople openly wondered if Zimmel hadn't been sneaking some holiday wine out of season. It was an extraordinary story and a very odd way for a holy man to behave. However, their disbelief so incensed the tailor that he took to screaming and swearing fiercely up and down. They had no choice but to change their minds. It was either that or watch the poor fellow burst every blood vessel in his head.

With Zimmel in command, everyone had something to do in preparation for the moment when the Baal Shem Tov would make his presence known. Even the non-Hasidic members of the community were involved, lending their own finest silverware and crockery to the festivities. For many, the atmosphere of cooperation in which old animosities were forgotten was the best proof that the Besht was among them. He had that effect on people.

Meir felt left out of the holiday mood that was sweeping the town. The appearance of the Besht now, so shortly after Meir's decision to give up his search for the fellow, made the shoemaker sorry. To assuage his sadness, he busied himself looking for Israel but, try as he might, his elusive cohort could not be found.

Giving up on his friend and doggedly returning to the cowshed, the shoemaker bumped into Sarah as she was coming out of her father's shop. The girl looked away. With a lump in his throat the size of an egg, Meir mumbled a greeting and raced by her, back to his quarters. There, leaning on his elbows and staring into the fire, was Israel.

"Why aren't you joining in the fun?" asked the shoemaker.

"Why aren't you?"

"It's not practical. I'm not for anything anymore that's not practical."

"Is love practical then?"

"What?"

"You can't fool me. That girl's been mooning around this shed for as long as I've been back."

"Really!"

"And I know you're planning something, a present for her, a pair of slippers or something."

"I wasn't planning any..."

"Sure, a pair of slippers. I know more than you think. If there's one thing that age teaches you, it's..."

"Why not? I could make her a pair of slippers for a wedding present. Does that bother you?"

"Me?" said the old man, curling up on the ground for a nap. "Why should it bother me?"

When Israel was asleep, Meir lit a candle and worked on the slippers. He became so involved in what he was doing that he worked throughout the evening, without stopping to eat, until he was finished. Then he slipped quietly out the door with the present. Returning several minutes later, without the slippers, Meir discovered that Israel had vanished again.

That night, after she shut the window of her room and undressed herself Sarah pulled down the covers of her bed and found Meir's slippers. They were glittering silver with little sparrows and flowers embroidered on them with black thread and beads of the deepest blue. Thinking them to be a gift from her father, she couldn't wait to try them on and was soon gliding about the floor in them, admiring their airy comfort.

Before she knew it, Sarah had passed through the doorway of her room and was walking naked in the darkness of her father's shop. She couldn't stop. Though she grabbed at her knees and flung herself from side to side, trying to fall, the slippers kept her upright and moving against her will. Approaching the door that led to the back of the shop, she had to push it open to avoid crashing into it.

Shivering in the night air, the girl wanted to call out but was too afraid. If she were to be seen like this, her life would be ruined. The cowshed loomed larger and larger. Sarah prayed that the strangers who lived there would be away.

Meanwhile, Meir sat warming his hands over the fire where a pot of tea was brewing. Having gotten used to his old friend's disappearances, he had put the fellow out of his mind. He was just picturing what Sarah's face would look like at the moment that she discovered the slippers when the shed door opened and there she was in the threshold, her face buried in her arms, her nakedness illuminated by the orange and yellow light of the flames.

Jumping to his feet, Meir kicked over the pot of tea. The fire sizzled from the encroaching moisture and flickered as Sarah, trying to hide her eyes, her breasts, and the black tuft of hair between her legs at once, continued to sail gently forward. When the fire went out, the dumbstruck shoemaker could still hear the soft pat of the slippers coming toward him until he felt Sarah's body come up against his. Lightly, he touched his hand to the trembling curve where her hip flowed into a slender leg. Sarah, grabbing Meir's fingers, found that they trembled as well.

"It's a nightmare," she wept and went on weeping as Meir tried desperately to soothe her, holding her and smoothing her hair.

"I'm not doing anything," he pleaded. "I won't, I promise."

She cried until she had no strength left to cry anymore. Then she buried her head under the young man's chin and clutched him tightly, letting his sobs replace her own. Finally, with no effort on either part, they lowered themselves to the floor.

Sarah had already gone by the time that Meir woke up in the morning. The only evidence of what had happened were the charred remains of the silver slippers. Inadvertently, they had been pushed onto the hot embers around the doused fire. Rolled up in a corner, snoring loudly, was old Israel.

Hearing voices from outside, the shoemaker crept to the door and listened. A group of men were standing at the back of the candle-maker's shop, discussing the town's disappointment at the failure of the Besht to show up as expected.

"That idiot, Zimmel, should be made to pay for all the work and expense himself," said the candle-maker.

"Where is that fellow?" asked one of the other men. "Has anyone seen him?"

"Hiding, no doubt," said another of the group.

"Last I heard," chuckled the candle-maker, "he was going all over town examining everyone's shoes."

All the men laughed, but none harder than the candle-maker as he continued.

"He's gone mad all right! Doesn't know what he's doing or what's going on around him!"

Moving away from the door, Meir sat back and tried to recapture the sight and sense of Sarah's body in his mind.

The shoemaker and the candle-maker's daughter met secretly all through the rest of the winter and Meir never felt better in his life. The bitter lines that had developed in his face melted away. He was constantly combing his hair and fluffing his beard, strolling about with a bit of a swagger, humming to himself, and taking care that his clothes were always clean and properly pressed.

"Ah, nothing like love to put dreams into the head of a practical man," old Israel might tease and Meir, waving him off, would deny it all with a big, irrepressible grin.

Hoping to glimpse his beloved as she worked, Meir would enter the candle-maker's shop often and peruse the various styles and colors of the candles. The candle-maker, suspicious of the young fellow who came so frequently and never made a single purchase, kept alert for anything that might be amiss. Sometimes, pretending that he had work to do in another room, the crafty father would leave the couple alone together and stand behind the door, listening for illicit conversation. But Meir and Sarah were too smart for him. They always waited for the candle-maker to be visibly busy before they slipped each other notes that would set the time and place of their next meeting.

Neglecting his work, Meir began to fall into silent reveries not unlike those he had experienced in the days preceding his journey. Only now, Sarah was the center of the fantastic world that materialized behind his eyes. She might be a giant, grown to the size of the earth itself and he, a renowned explorer traveling across her mysterious landscape, entering dark pathways, seeking out the most hidden areas of her sensual terrain. At other times he was the master of vast armies and countless ships, kneeling at her feet, placing his immense power and his own life in the service of her slightest whim. Or she could become an ethereal creature, translucent against an azure sky, walking green meadows in a rain of lilac petals.

Whatever the vision that came into Meir's mind, it became so precious to him that he couldn't bear the thought of losing it. He preserved them by scribbling them down on scraps of paper. In this way he not only sustained his fancies, he lived them, in a sense, by being with his love in new ways every day even when she wasn't there. Each of his jottings, as he was writing them down, inspired new thoughts and pictures that sprang from his heart like reflections escaping from a mirror. Sketchy notes expanded, broke open, and shattered like clay vessels left sitting too close to a flame; each glowing shard a moment of internal experience suspended in time, striking a single note in an endless song of love. Meir kissed every page before hiding it beneath a log in the cowshed.

With Meir so preoccupied, no money was coming in. Israel, despite his happiness at his young friend's exalted state, became dismayed.

"We need some cash," he complained.

"Why don't you make some," replied the shoemaker.

"Me? I'm old! We'll starve!"

"You're supposed to be a healer; go make some medicine and heal somebody."

"With the herbs they have around here?"

"Fake!"

"Is that a way to talk? I'd be lucky to cure a stuffy nose with the weeds that grow..."

"How would you know? You don't go out during

the day! It's like you're afraid of..."

"I go out! Never you mind! Only I'm invisible when I go. You can't be too careful."

"That's what I mean! What do you have to be careful for?"

"Uhhh...Sprites! That's it! This town is crowded with them!"

"What are you talking about? Where?"

"Everywhere! Trust me; I can spot them. Age teaches you that," insisted the old man, tiptoeing around the shed, looking in corners, kicking at the haystack, peaking under the bedrolls and in Meir's tool sack.

"What do these sprites want with you?"

"Wandering healers; they hate us! How would you feel if you were a sprite, working hard at making mischief, making cows go dry, giving people itchy rashes to disturb their sleep, and along comes some old man who fixes everything up? You'd be pretty annoyed, that's what!"

"So disguise yourself!"

"What? Trick a sprite? They invented the word! You might know about ships..."

"All right."

"...but sprites are my territory and I can tell you, trying to outfox a sprite is like wrestling with a rose-bush; you can think you have the upper hand..."

"All right."

"...but who gets stuck? Now, becoming invisible is another matter. It's defensive. When in doubt, a low profile..."

"All right, all right, all right," said Meir, grabbing his tools and heading for the door.

Though Meir tried not to think about it, the day of Sarah's marriage approached rapidly. He couldn't imagine her with that weasel-faced beadle, Lutik, and it wasn't until preparations had begun that he realized that he could lose her. By then, Sarah was so busy that she had no time for the shoemaker. Excused from working in her father's shop, she became impossible to reach. It was already the night before the ceremony when Meir got so desperate that he sailed a rock through the shuttered window of her room. Moments later, Sarah stepped out of her house and Meir pulled her into a shadowy section of the garden.

"What's the matter with you? You'll wake up the town," she said.

"Break the match."

"And sin against my father? Haven't we sinned enough?"

"Sinned? I haven't sinned; have you sinned? You call it a sin?"

"I think you woke my father."

"I don't care if..."

"I do! I'm getting married tomorrow!"

"You're already married! To me!"

"Explain *that* to my father."

"You love *me*!"

"So what? I'm talking marriage here. It was all arranged before we met."

"It can be changed."

"And what about the new house that Lutik bought? You should have seen how happy he was. Such a beautiful house! And a big, wonderful garden!"

"We're a match."

"I'm already matched."

"Break the match!"

"A match is a match!"

Pushing Meir away from her, Sarah ran back to her house, slamming the door behind her before Meir could get in. The shoemaker begged at the keyhole, but she did not answer. Downtrodden, he headed home to the cowshed. As he drew close to it, Meir heard a good deal of rustling going on inside.

"What are you doing now, you old clown?" he called. "I thought you forgot about looking for sprites."

But it was not Israel whom Meir met as he entered; it was the candle-maker, wild-eyed and soaked with perspiration, quivering like the cover of a boiling pot of stew. The tips of his fingers yellowed by pressure, the candle-maker held up a clenched fist out of which Meir's hidden scraps of paper protruded like torn and wrinkled accusers. Before he could speak, the shoemaker caught a blow across the nose and went down. The candle-maker commenced beating him about the back with both fists. Lunging for the man's legs, Meir tripped him and, first grabbing hold of his tools, ran for his life. He didn't stop until he was out of the town.

Meir set up camp near the river and wondered what had become of Israel. Hoping that the candle-maker wouldn't take out his anger on the old fellow, the shoemaker figured that there was nothing he could do but wait. Days went by with Meir nursing his battered nose and weeping at the thought of losing Sarah. Still, when he remembered making love to her, it made him feel good. At least it did until Rachel came to mind. He was thinking about her now too. Going back to Warsaw was out of the question.

Just when Meir had about given up on the old fellow, Israel arrived one afternoon with a broad-brimmed hat that sat so low on his head that it hid his face, and wearing black stockings over his shoes. The shoemaker, running to greet his friend with a powerful hug, nearly knocked the fellow over.

"Easy," said the old man. "A little less glad and a bit more gentle!"

"I didn't know what happened to you."

"We sure left in a hurry, didn't we?"

"Where have you been? Why are you dressed like that?"

"Shhhh, there's a crazy man after me. He's been following me for days."

"Why didn't you make yourself invisible?" laughed the shoemaker.

"That's not funny. Staying invisible is hard work. I'm not so young anymore. So I decided your disguise idea wasn't so bad. One thing that age teaches you is you're never too old to learn a new trick so long as it's an easy one. That goes for both men and dogs. Where do we go now?"

"Medzhibozh, I guess."

"The Besht? You've changed your mind again? I don't know what you expect out of him; never trust a holy man is what I say."

"I thought you liked him."

"That has nothing to do with it. If you'd take my advice, you'd forget about him. Stop worrying so much. But if you'd rather hear it from somebody famous, that's fine with me. Who am I? An old man. I think it's foolish, but so what? I'll go along, but don't ask me why."

"I've got to go. I can't go home the same nothing as when I started."

"Never mind. I'm old. I don't understand 'nothing.' He's supposed to be a handsome fellow, so let's go look. And what happened to your nose?"

"The candle-maker's fist," replied Meir, slinging his tools over his shoulder.

"Well, he fixed it. It doesn't point left anymore," said Israel as he pulled off the black stockings and tossed them away. "It still twists a little, but it ends up straight enough."

"I thought you needed those stockings for your disguise. What about the crazy man?"

"They're hard to walk in and we have to hurry. You know, the Besht is pretty old himself."

Then, locking arms, the old man with the bright orange shoes and the young shoemaker with the twisted nose recharted their course toward the famous teacher who, it was suspected by one of them, was very good looking.

8 🐦

BEING ON THE ROAD HEARTENED MEIR. AFTER
all, it was spring and early mornings like this one,
when the soft fragrance that the dew unlocked from
the young grass worked upon him like a tonic, were
the best of all. He could breathe deeper, feeling the
pops and crackles of his rib cage as it spread like
wings over his expanding lungs. With a wide, pleasant stretch of his limbs, all the aches and stiffness
from sleeping on the ground fled as readily as children from their beds. There was no trace of heart-
ache left in him, only a gentle gratitude for the
warm touch of sunlight on his face and, now that
Medzhibozh was no more than a week away, a longing to find the Besht at last.

Israel was still asleep and Meir watched over him.
The old fellow seemed to have aged considerably in
the days since they had left Lvov. His cheeks had
hollowed and paled to a yellowish white. Even his
eyes looked dimmer lately, as if the color were slowly
draining out of them. At present, the only hint of
life in the man was his robust snore. That at least,

thought the shoemaker, was a good sign.

Letting his friend sleep, Meir returned to his old habit of watching the clouds. The heavens were swarming with shapes. Flying horses turned into dancing cows, toothy dragons rolled in on themselves and performed somersaults, floating fish with oddly shaped hats became lithe and seductive maidens; all changing rapidly and easily, without a pause. Directly above Meir, a human figure formed, its arms extending east and west for miles, its head as big as a mountain. There were empty spaces where the eyes should have been, through which the sky peeked blue and radiant.

Reminded of the clay man, Meir thought of how much alike he and the monster had been. They had both gotten a lot that they hadn't looked for. Maybe that's all there is for anyone. You tread water, trying to keep your head above the surface, and take hold of whatever drifts by. Someday, if you're lucky, a wave or a current pushes you to shore. Or maybe there is no current; just an endless alternation between surge and calm in which people exhaust themselves for no reason. At least in sinking, the bottom was a certainty you could touch. Then, coming up again, who knows how different the world might appear. If only someone had thought of setting a boat on the waters, one with colored sails that could be seen from far off.

With that kind of hope, one might brave anything.

As the giant cloud figure came apart, Meir tried to see the faces of those he loved in the scattering white puffs. He couldn't do it. Things were taking shape, but he could no longer make out what they were. Closing his eyes, he attempted to draw a picture of Rachel out of his memory and failed. No matter how hard he concentrated, there was always something a trifle off; the distance between the eyes, the exact angle of the nose. He couldn't get it straight and had to settle on an image of a face and body that, while not perfectly Rachel, at least resembled her. Then he began to wish the clothes away.

"Hey you, Ship-maker! That's quite a look you have on your face!" called Israel, snapping Meir out of his reverie.

The old man stood up, rubbing his arms and legs, pouring some water into his hat, and then washing his face in it.

"And what were you thinking of?" he continued coyly.

"Nothing," answered Meir. "No... I was thinking about the Besht, what he'll be like when we see him."

"He'll be old, what else? If I were your age, I'd be dreaming of women. In fact, I have been anyway. Hundreds of them. Beautiful fat ones with tiny bird's feet like the goyim paint and put in their churches.

Wonderful! That's what should be on your mind. Take it from me, there are three pains a fellow shouldn't be without; good books to break his brains, good work to break his back, and a good woman to break his 'you know what.'"

"Heart?"

"More or less. Women kill you, but it makes life worth living. They're very important to a man; them and a beard."

"A beard?"

"For beauty! A man without his beard is like a cat without its fur. Who wants to look? Why, to shave it off would be a sin. It's a gift from God. It proclaims the man. It tells you the kind of fellow he is, how much experience he's had, even what he likes to eat. And useful? Its uses are innumerable! It keeps you warm in the winter and holds moisture in the summer. It's something for people to look at while they're talking to you and for children to admire. It helps you think! How many great rabbis have made breakthroughs in Torah while twirling the ends of their beards in their fingers? It's staggering! A beard is something to pull on when you're angry, to wring when you're grief-stricken, and to fluff when you're in love. That's most important, love. Because, first and foremost, a beard is a thing of beauty."

Lifting his hands so that their tops pushed up his

whiskers and the backs of his fingers pressed against either side of his chin, Israel danced around the amused shoemaker and sang.

Praise to the Lord who in his wisdom placed
These flowing strands upon my face,
That tickle in my true love's ear
And warn her that my lips are near.

Looking on in delight, Meir forgot all of his concerns over his friend's health. So what if the fellow has lost a little weight? Anyone who can jig like that at his age, singing songs to his beard, must be in fine fettle.

"That's what the world is," Israel went on, "the whiskers on the face of the infinite and a man is either a flea or a butterfly in it. Think about it. There are things I could teach you."

"Uh huh, but right now don't you think we should get going. We've a good distance to Medzhibozh yet and..."

"The Besht, the Besht, the Besht! Always the Besht! What do you know about him? Hearsay! Good! Have it your way! It's not a problem! I can talk as we walk; I'll tell you a story."

"Oh God, I don't need a story," complained Meir, starting ahead.

"You don't? Then you don't need to live! Everything is a story! All you know of the Besht is from stories! Your life is a story, and whose isn't? We make them up every day, only most of us can't tell the difference between a romantic tragedy and a clown show! And you don't need a story? The universe is God's story!"

"I thought it was his beard."

"It's both! Now listen, I know a story about a fellow who got into trouble telling a story about a storyteller who told him stories that he retold with ulterior purposes."

"Oh, no."

"He was called Saykle. His real name was Tsaykle, but he had spent time in England and it went to his head. When he returned, he insisted that everyone call him Saykle. A poor exchange, but what can you do? He wouldn't answer to anything else.

"Now, this Saykle was a barber. A terrible one. As blind as a new potato, he was always cutting or gouging someone. He had to put his nose up against the customer's head just to see what he was doing. And the hairs tickled him. So when he wasn't sticking someone, he was sneezing all over them. The men of his village both hated and feared him.

"You'd think he'd starve, right? A barber like that? But not at all; the women loved him. Tall, slight, frail-looking, he was just their type. Women love that kind. It makes them feel motherly and lusty all at once. This barber had a big influence on them. They'd drag in their husbands and sons for more haircuts than they had hairs. By the ears! All for no purpose but so that they, these ladies, could have the pleasure of watching this string bean Saykle do his work. The favored spot to stand was right behind him where they could fix their eyes on the skinny bottom that stuck up, wiggled, and swayed as he nearsightedly hacked up their males.

"The end result of all this barbering, as you may have guessed, Ship-maker, was a growing number of bald men about. That barber would just cut and cut until there wasn't anything left to cut. It became a fashion. And the men didn't mind that part of it themselves. You see, they realized that it was safer to have one's head polished than to have to cope with the barber's sharp scissors. Unfortunately, the powders he used on their gleaming scalps made him sneeze all the more. But you take the good with the bad and in time, the town came to be known as 'The Village of Bald Men.'"

"Please!" cried Meir, holding his hands to his ears and trying to outpace Israel. "What do I care about sneezing barbers and bald men?"

"It's background material. A thing is only as good

as its foundation. I'm building you one. So this Saykle…"

"You're giving me a headache! Can't we walk in peace? There's a lot of ground to cover."

"Sure, sure, and the story will help. It'll make time go so fast you won't even see it pass. A story can do that. And it may teach you something, clear your head."

"There's nothing I want to learn from you!"

"About women," winked the old man.

"I know about women!"

"One! You know about one woman! That one who threw you over in Lvov! This will teach you about *all* women. It may come in handy when you go back to your Warsaw girlfriend."

"If you have to, get on with it!"

"So this Saykle, like I said, was a rotten barber, but he was no ignoramus. He knew who was buttering his bread and on which side. His business depended on the women. He had to hold their interest. Their husbands loathed him and were looking for any opportunity to get rid of him. Them, he had to keep preoccupied. They were mad enough over the haircuts. If they were to notice any other funny business…Well, I'll tell you, it was a worry for the barber.

"Dealing with the wives was easy at first. All

Saykle had to do was what he was already doing, occasionally giving something a little extra like wiping his hands on the seat of pants, or dropping a towel so that he could bend over to pick it up. Things like that enchanted those females, and they were completely under his spell. The men were another matter. The situation with them was very delicate. One wrong move on the barber's part could turn the bright sunshine of his prosperity into a rain of blows. So far, they suspected nothing."

"This is ridiculous," said Meir. "How could they not be suspicious? What did they think about all those haircuts?"

"Good grooming. What should they think? We're not discussing whores here. These were respectable wives, modest and virtuous to the breaking point. Every one of them would have denied any motive other than the good looks of their families. Even to themselves!"

"Couldn't the men see what was happening..."

"Right under their noses! That's where it was happening all right, and it got worse. Some of the women were so struck by certain of the barber's particularly provocative poses that they gasped and sighed out loud. He had to keep talking to cover it up. The weather, politics, descriptions of the various shapes of people's heads, whatever came into his mind found a voice. It worked for awhile. Saykle was so boring that the men drowsed, leaving the barber to pump and wave his backside as much as he liked. But, as it turned out, he was too boring. Despite the inspiration that his bottom afforded them, the women began to nod as well, jeopardizing everything Saykle had worked for.

"Now Saykle was hard pressed to come up with something to say to keep the wives awake. He had no imagination. He did, however, have an adventure once, while he was in England, and it was an adventure that would have made a fascinating story. But it was so sordid and mysterious that he was afraid to tell it except as a last resort. It involved a street woman as large as two men and fatter than a cow, who always sat in an alley between a rough sailor's bar and a windowless, brick building that served as a prison for the insane. There, beneath an umbrella of rags, enthroned on a pile of flower-patterned pillows that had faded from sun and rain, the tawny wench wove tales for the coppers of anyone who would listen. She called herself 'Garette,' and never moved from that spot.

"'His Majesty, Sweet Jesus, allow but so many footsteps to each wretched child of man,' she was known to say, pronouncing each syllable separately and distinctly as was her way, 'and I saving mine all up so as I never die.'

"The beggars in the neighborhood took care of her every need; washing her down when she was dirty, combing her hair after the rain and wind had knotted it, emptying her jars of excrement. For her part, she shared the money she earned telling stories with them, bestowing coins like royal gifts. Whatever she saved she placed on the pillow directly under her, alongside her other valuables; a wooden cross and the key to a weathered trunk that she kept at her side. You might think, Ship-maker, that sitting on all that stuff was a terrible discomfort to her, but what can I tell you? The story says it wasn't. Her regal posture never wavered."

"Hold it!" shouted Meir. "You're tangling me all up! What happened to the barber? Where did this fat woman who thinks she's a queen come from?"

"But she really was a queen!" protested Israel. "Or a princess rather. The last survivor of her tribe. They were an island folk who were known as 'The Fruit People' because their women, when they got pregnant, would climb into the trees and stay there until they delivered their babies into hammocks that were hung from the branches. They were descendants of ancient Egyptian fishermen who…"

"You're making this up!"

"Absolutely not! Look!" insisted Israel, pushing

the hair off of his forehead and pointing to a scar above his right eye. "I got this and the story directly from the barber."

"I thought you said that he wouldn't tell this story!"

"A patient man gets to see the pot boil. It got to the point where he had to tell it. One afternoon, while Saykle was going on and on about the advantages of fine-toothed combs over horsehair brushes, the women, one by one, joined their dozing husbands. The entire shop inhaled and exhaled with the gurgles and whistles of repose. One old woman, gagging on her own saliva, awakened suddenly, grabbed her husband by the nose, and dragged him out of the shop, slapping a few of the other ladies awake as she passed. Soon, all of the women were up, rubbing their eyes and grumbling.

"Desperate, the barber started twisting his body into dangerously obscene poses, thrusting his bottom almost into the face of one woman, indiscreetly scratching his loins for another. He winked, made squeaky kissing noises through pursed lips, and undid the top buttons of his shirt, unveiling a smooth, hairless chest. It was a disgrace. But he did have some success. Two of the women went into trances, one swooned, another fell to her knees and, wrapping her arms around the barber's legs, pressed her cheek tightly to his backside.

"Still, there were five women who, in their sleepy stupor, did not respond at all. Stumbling noisily about the shop, they started to stir the men. Everything that Saykle had built was on the verge of being destroyed. He had no other choice but to take a chance and tell the story of his adventure with the female, Garette. And do you know, Ship-maker, it worked like a wonder. A calm descended on the room. The waking men remained glued to their seats and listened along with the women, who divided their own attention between the barber's words and his appealing figure."

"God in heaven, protect me!" exclaimed Meir.

"Are you going to let me finish before I die of old age?"

"Finish!"

"Good! So the barber told his story about this Garette who was a big attraction. People came from all over to hear her tales and the barber, open to new experiences as travelers sometimes are, was no exception. He saw a crowd, was curious, and investigated. At the center of the massing people, her hands on her folded knees, sat the enchantress, unfolding one bizarre yarn after the other, speaking in hushed tones so that her listeners had to lean intimately forward. The barber was impressed. Returning time and time again, he and the storyteller were soon quite familiar to each other.

"Eventually, Garette asked him to come at late hours, when no one else was around, and she would tell him tales that were for his ears alone. The devouring look in her eyes as she made the offer, frightened Saykle. But he wanted to hear the stories, so he agreed to come that very night.

"'You make love to me now,' hissed Garette when the barber arrived. He refused and, taking note of the woman's powerful size, made sure to stay outside of the reach of her arms. Laughing, she picked up a stone from the ground, rubbed it gently with her fingers, and licked it with the edges and tip of her tongue.

"I don't need to tell you the uproar this part of the story started in the barber's shop. The men protested that it wasn't fit to be told in front of the women. The women disagreed. Pulling at the dampened underarms of their dresses, patting their own flustered faces, they insisted that a story was, after all, only a story and nothing to get excited about."

"Why are you torturing me?" moaned Meir.

"Anyway, the wives got their husbands under control and the barber continued, explaining that he would have run away the moment Garette made her intentions plain, had it not been for the magic of her voice and the tale she began to spin.

"She told of a remarkably beautiful woman who was so vain that she prayed night and day to be able to show herself before multitudes. Her prayers were answered and she was made to float through the air, over all the towns and cities of the world. Populations rushed into the streets at the sight of her, pointing and shouting praises. In some places, people hoisted flags to her; in others, they rang bells. Choirs sang to her as she hove into sight. Men wept in the trees and on the rooftops. Love-struck youths planted daggers in themselves over her unreachability. It all seemed marvelous to the woman.

"Then there came a day when, drifting over a land of high, rolling hills, she spotted a boy atop one of them. He was sitting by himself and playing a flute. It was the first time that she had ever been moved by the beauty of someone aside from herself. The music of his flute seemed to enter her. She called to him but he was so far below her, and with the playing of his music, he did not hear.

"Round and round the earth she went and every time she passed that hilltop, it was the same thing. Though she called as loudly as she could, and waved her arms and legs, nothing would attract his attention. She even wished that she could leave the sky and stand next to the boy. Holding her breath, she dangled in the air, thinking heavy thoughts, but it was impossible. A person can't get every prayer answered whenever they want. She got depressed. The flute-player so occupied her mind that she no longer noticed the mobs of admirers who continued to cheer as she flew over them. All that mattered to her was when she would next pass the boy's hill.

"Finally it happened that, as the woman gazed upon him from the sky, she could no longer bear the distance between herself and the boy. Tears dropped from her eyes, and some of these tears landed on the young flute-player's head. He stopped his playing. The woman was overjoyed. Now he would look up, see her, and be as taken by her beauty as everyone else. If only she could be with him at that moment, lying alongside of him on the cool grass. But when the boy lifted his face, all that greeted her was an empty stare. His eyes were dead, blind, and raising them had been a useless gesture made in complete darkness.

"Weeping more pitiably than ever, the woman floated away beyond the hills. After that, at a certain hour on certain days, the boy remembered to stop his flute-playing and wait for the strange, warm rain. Lifting his face, he would try to catch its salty drops on his tongue.

"When Garette finished the tale, she took out her

146 ～

key, unlocked her chest, and placed the stone that she had been rubbing and fingering in it.

"'For every tale I tell you, a stone go in the box,' she said to the barber, pointing long, sharp, fingernails at a spot between his legs. 'At the instant it is filled, I will have you and, so as you never forget, I put my mark on you, too.' Then she pressed her wooden cross to her lips and kissed it three times."

"The end!" begged Meir. "You're drowning me with words! I'm sinking! Sunk!"

"Don't interrupt," said the old man. "I'm just getting to the good part. After she put her cross away, Garette gave the barber a big smile that showed all of her black teeth and, taking one of her breasts in each hand, squeezed and shook them in front of him. It scared him, so he ran. But he came back the next night and again and again to hear her. And every night it was the same thing; another story and another stone.

"Imagine, if you can, Ship-maker, how taken the women of the village were with Saykle's story. They were more attracted to the fellow than ever. Many of them sensed the danger of their infatuation, but they couldn't help themselves. Day after day, they dragged their husbands and sons in for trims so that they, these feverish wives, could hear another tale that the barber had learned from the street woman. For each story, with Garette's knife-like fingernails in their minds, and while the focus of their stolen glances shifted from Saykle's backside to the front of his pants, they counted another stone, waiting, tense and expectant, to discover whether she had actually marked him.

"It was different for the men. They lost interest in the barber's stories. They had other things to think about. Because of all the time they were forced to spend in the barber's shop, their businesses were going to ruin. Some grew suspicious that there was more to this madness of the wives than an obsession for clean-cut males. But what could they do about it? The slightest complaint from a husband and the wife would harangue him for hours, cursing his ingratitude, calling him names like 'Onion-head' and 'Sheep-face,' howling that he loved his hair more than he loved the mother of his children. Asking for a day off from going to the barber was asking to get slapped in the head. A careless whimper could win an icy glare and lonely nights.

"But things couldn't go on like that forever. The pressure that these women were under from their own corruptions, Ship-maker, was enormous. Lust and curiosity make a strange sandwich. The more you chew it, the harder it is to swallow. And the taste of it just hints at being so good that you can't help but take more and more bites until you have to find a way to get it down before you choke.

"So what did these wives do? They began to ask the barber over to their homes while their husbands were out. Of course, he accepted. At first, he mistook the requests for emergency calls; a head of hair in drastic need of clipping, a bald pate that cried out for a gloss. However, it did not take him long to find out that was not the case. At each home he was greeted by a wife who pulled him to the floor, hiked up her dress, and caught his hips with her knees. From the first incident, he was terribly puzzled. If he gave in to the temptation, he would be in greater danger from the husbands than ever. Furthermore, an outright refusal might insult the woman in question and cause her to withdraw her support of his shop. So what do you think the fellow did?"

"I don't know," moaned the shoemaker.

"He pretended that he didn't know what was going on. Clever, eh? Very matter-of-factly, he took out his scissors and set to work trimming the presented tuft of feminine hair. He did it with all of them. Shrieking as he accidentally jabbed them, each wife in turn was too embarrassed to point out the error that he was making. Call it vanity, or call it modesty; it's the same thing. When he had done his business, they simply gave him the money that he asked for, bid him good-bye, and stood staring at the lopsided triangles and irregular circles of hair beneath their bellies as he went on his way. But the barber had made one very grave oversight."

"Don't tell me," said Meir. "The husbands noticed what he had done to their wives and chased him out of the village."

"Exactly!"

"Wonderful. And then what?"

"And then nothing. That's it."

"No, no, no, you're cutting it too short. That can't be it."

"What else do you want? That's it. The barber's gone."

"That's the big finish! You're crazy! And your story stinks!"

"Don't be so harsh. If a story affects you, if it gets you thinking, then..."

"There's nothing to think about with a story that stupid!"

"Are you sure? A story can be a sly thing. It can get under your skin."

"What happened to that barber?!"

"Who knows? All I know is that the husbands divorced their wives and left to start a village of their own. The new settlement came to be known as 'The Village of Lonely, Hairy Men,' but that's another story."

"Well, did that Garette ever put her mark on him?"

"They threw the barber out of town before he got to that part."

"Lousy, lousy, lousy. I'm supposed to learn something from such a mishmash? What? That if a woman opens her legs for me, I shouldn't give her a haircut?"

"That's not bad."

"That I'm a moron for listening to you?"

"If you like."

"That people who tell rotten stories should keep their mouths shut?"

Israel sniffed and shrugged, and walked on ahead of the shoemaker. Meir was ready to hurl another insult at him when he realized again how drawn the old fellow had become. Surely, Israel was more ill than he was letting on. Rather than aggravate his friend's condition, Meir relented. In any case, frustrating as it was, the story had helped to pass the time. It was nearly dusk.

Walking along behind the old man, the shoemaker made up several endings of his own to the tale of the barber, and he found each one of them to be superior to the original. His favorite was the one in which he had Saykle falling for Garette's old trick of softening her voice. While he was leaning in to hear her better, she got him in her clutches, swallowed him whole into her arms where he was overcome by a thick, overly sweet aroma, like rotting pears, that rose from her skin, and instantly excited by the exotic flutterings of her fingers in his trousers. With swift precision, her thumb flicked and its nail found its mark.

Meir could see the women of the barber's village running from the shop, horrified by Saykle's description of savage sexual rites. The husbands, scared witless as well, sprouted new growth on their scalps that stood straight up and reached for the ceiling. And this sight, in turn, frightened the barber. His eyes bugged out, curing his nearsightedness and, the best part, he bit off half of his tongue. He could never tell another story. In the end, the wives returned to being good and wholesome wives, never going near the barber again. The men only went for haircuts when they wanted them, which was rare enough. But when they did, they went to a barber who now stuck to his trade, plying it to his own best ability which in time turned out to be quite good. Meir liked a happy ending.

Pleased with himself, the young shoemaker listened to the gentle weeping of the wind in the trees and was soothed by a few warm drops of rain that fell on his face. That night, he dreamed of Rachel. They were walking together in a dark field beneath a starry sky. On their arms were shoe-shaped baskets filled with wildflowers and mushrooms that they had gathered. She looked perfect.

9 🐚

AS THE NEXT SEVERAL DAYS PROGRESSED, Israel's health worsened. He stopped taking solid food, subsisting instead on thin broth and bits of moistened bread. Blue-black folds developed under his eyes, half covering them as they sank into their sockets. His skin shriveled and his veined hands hung like weights on his withered arms. And yet, his pace never slackened. On the contrary, his steps gained urgency the closer the two friends came to their destination, Medzhibozh, the home of the Besht.

"We're wasting too much time," the old fellow complained. Like stopping to eat; why do that? We can eat as we walk."

"If you don't slow down, you'll kill us both," countered Meir.

"Slow down? When we're almost there?"

"The Besht isn't going to die before we arrive."

"I hope not! But why take chances? You're the one who wants to see him anyway."

"Not if it means walking ourselves to death."

"Dying! Death! Fine conversation to be starting

with an old man! How would you like it if I talked about women all the time?"

"You do!"

"So let that be a lesson to you. Besides, you can't walk yourself to death. Death doesn't stay in one place long enough for that. *It* finds *you* and not the other way around. Sometimes you can hear it coming, but..."

"I only meant that you're pushing yourself too hard."

"Me? The shoes are doing all the work. They're remarkable!"

As Israel pressed on with fresh gusto, Meir tagged along from behind. Looking at the shoes on the old man's feet, their bright orange color showing through the accumulated layers of dirt and dust, the shoemaker almost believed that they did indeed possess magical qualities. The two friends didn't stop to rest until well after dark when they finally made camp and settled in for the night.

The next morning, the shoemaker discovered that the old man had vanished again. Only this time, Israel had left a note behind, stuck in the band of the broad-brimmed hat that the fellow had picked up in Lvov.

"Couldn't wait," read Meir. "See you when I do."

Although Meir was used to his companion's unexpected disappearances, the old fellow had never before left such a message behind and it worried him. Maybe it was a joke.

"All right," called the shoemaker, getting to his feet, "stop playing invisible with me."

In that instant, two hands took hold of Meir's shoulders and flung him back to the ground. Before he could utter a cry, the full weight of a man came down across his chest, pressing him flat, folding and pinning his arms beneath the bony knees of the assailant. A hand pinched his face and thrust his jaw up so that the shoemaker's cheeks were caught in his own teeth.

"Where is he?" demanded the attacker.

Filthy, matted hair dangled in Meir's face, and the stranger's fur-stuffed ears wiggled wildly as he took the shoemaker's throat in his fingers.

"Zimmel!" choked Meir, recognizing the Lvov tailor by his ears, but the obviously deranged man did not respond except to tighten his hold on the shoemaker's neck.

"Where is he? Where?" persisted Zimmel as Meir fought for air, his pulse pounding in his temples.

The world seemed, to Meir, to recede, leaving the fierce eyes of the madman floating and flashing as they came toward him like flames in the eye sockets of an invisible fish. Those eyes reminded Meir of another pair he had seen, a pair that belonged to a question-eating criminal of a Lublin fishmonger. They gave Meir an idea. With a tremendous effort, he wrenched his hands free from under Zimmel's knees and pried loose the fingers that were digging into his neck.

"He's where he's hiding!" Meir retched, pulling his answer from the tailor's question.

Zimmel relaxed his hold and peered at his prisoner.

"And you'll take me to him?"

"Of course," replied the shoemaker, weak with fatigue, without a notion of whom they were talking about.

"I'll have my proof!"

"Without a doubt."

"But you were with him. I've been following you. And now you'll lead me to him?"

"Sure," said Meir, realizing that it was old Israel that the mad tailor was after. "He got away from me. I'd like to get my hands on him myself."

"What do you want him for?"

"Me? Uh...for...for proof! What else?"

"Yes, proof. Or people call you an imbecile, go to other shops, laugh until they're blue. They don't care that they drive you into poverty, starve your children. Proof! Or keep your mouth shut about what you know!"

"That's people for you," agreed Meir. "They can have something right in front of them, and they don't believe it unless they see it. It's disgusting!"

"They'll see," mumbled the tailor as he got up off the shoemaker. "A Besht is a Besht and I know one when I see one...That's that...Dumb color for shoes ...Where's he gonna hide in shoes like those...I'll get him and, when I do, they'll see and that'll be that. Settled."

"So that was it," thought Meir. "He thinks the old man is the Besht. That's what created that stir in Lvov. Lunacy!"

While Meir caught his breath, Zimmel started rifling through the shoemaker's sack, gobbling down every morsel of food that he could find. Then, finding a fine new pair of shoes, the tailor quickly exchanged them for the beat up pair that he had on.

"Hey, what do you think you're doing?" called Meir, shocked that the tailor, a fellow tradesman, knew no better than to take without paying. A tugging contest ensued in which both fellows pulled at the sack with all of their might, spilling much of its contents. Among the shoemaker's things that fell to the ground, was a small jar of orange dye.

"Aha!" shouted Zimmel as he let go of the sack to scoop up the jar and raise it above his head.

"Evidence!"

"Try not to get excited," soothed Meir, backing away from the maniac who waved a fist at him with renewed malevolence. "Keep the shoes. No charge."

When the tailor lifted a foot to charge him, the shoemaker doubled over and protected his head with his arms. But the attack didn't come. Instead, Zimmel took a step backward. Each man was more confused than the other. The tailor tried again to bring the disobedient foot forward and, this time, the other foot moved, stepping effortlessly backward of its own accord. Screaming at the top of his lungs, beating the sides of his head, writhing his hips, Zimmel grunted and tried to lunge for the shoemaker with no result but a rapid succession of steps in the opposite direction. At last, in an effort to outsmart his feet, the wily fellow pivoted on his heels and attempted walking backwards. Immediately, his feet stepped bravely forward. The shoemaker looked on as his would-be attacker fought against his own legs which, nevertheless, carried the man further and further away.

"And if you don't like orange, who cares?" yelled Meir as soon as the tailor was a safe distance away and almost out of view. "I do! So go bang your head on a rock! Get cholera! It's an excellent color and you can go crap in the ocean!"

With the tailor gone, Meir sat down to collect his

thoughts. Zimmel had been so sure that Israel was the Besht that he had driven himself mad with the idea. And hadn't the old man acted rather strange in Lvov, refusing to be seen, all that nonsense about sprites. And that disguise he wore! Was it possible? All that talk about the Besht being so good a fellow and how handsome he was...It was possible! That crook! He was the Besht! What kind of game was he playing, taking advantage of people, pretending to be a no one when he was a big someone.

Then Meir began to weep. He had had the Besht with him all the time and never knew it. Pals or not, Israel would never help him now. He didn't deserve help. He was too stupid. Maybe it was a test and he had failed. He could never go home now. How could he expect Rachel to marry someone as stupid as he was.

But what had happened to the old man? He was still missing. What if he were lost and delirious? He hadn't been well at all. What if he were lying helpless somewhere, dying? What if he fell into the hands of brigands? How could he protect himself at his age and in his condition?

Meir tried to run in every direction at once, frantically calling Israel's name, circling every tree, poking his head into every patch of shrubbery. When no sign of the old man turned up by nightfall, the shoemaker convinced himself that Israel had abandoned him on purpose, preferring a lonely death to the company of so stupid a companion. He was probably dead already.

Friendless, homeless, with barely more than two rubles in his pocket, a downcast Meir broke camp. The nearest town was Medzhibozh. Someone had to go there and tell the holy man's friends and family that the great teacher had died on the road, fleeing the incontinent dimwittedness of an unworthy acquaintance. Who, figured Meir, was better suited to the task than the oaf in question. So, plodding on in the clear, liquid moonlight, the shoemaker aimed his nose in the direction of the destination that he had so long yearned for and which now held no promise for him at all.

Medzhibozh was a small town, no different from countless others that were part of the landscape of Poland. Low, clumsily patched roofs sat on the squat wood-framed houses. Tiny gardens near the front doors, and flower pots that were nailed beneath windows, brightened the grey faces of the homes with splashes of pink, violet, green, and white. When Meir arrived, the milkman was making his rounds, his cart clacking and creaking as it rolled along.

Meir stopped to get his bearings and a young man

ran up to him out of nowhere.

"Are you the ship-maker?" asked the fellow.

"What did you call me?"

"Are you the ship-maker that the Master is expecting?"

"Ship-maker! He's alive!" Meir shouted, grabbing the young man by the hands and swinging him around. "Alive! He's alive!"

The young man pulled free of the shoemaker's grip, straightened his clothes, and smoothed his hair before resuming the conversation with the excitable stranger.

"Then you *are* the ship-maker?"

"Anything you like!"

"The Master asked me to welcome you in his name," the man spoke as if reciting the text of a prepared script, impressing Meir with the seriousness of his tone. "He has just recently returned from one of his journeys and, since he is planning to leave on another shortly, he wishes to see you as soon as possible. There is a service that he would like to ask of you. Regretfully, he has no money and hopes that you will accept his blessing in place of payment."

"A service? Of me? Of course! Whatever it is! And he'll bless me? A blessing from the Baal Shem is worth more than a hundred fortunes! Tell him I'll be right there!"

162 ∽

After the young man left, the shoemaker rummaged through his sack, looking for something to give his old friend as a present. There was nothing that would do, so Meir began a search that led him into every shop in the awakening village, offering all of his two rubles and six kopeks to anyone who could provide him with a gift worthy enough to be given to the Baal Shem Tov. In a town as poor as Medzhibozh, even the measly sum of two rubles and six kopeks was nothing to sneeze at.

Parading their finest and most unusual wares before the shoemaker, the shopkeepers did everything they could to interest him in a purchase. There was a sealskin coat from Siberia that still had the seal's head attached, serving as a hood. Meir didn't like that. Another fellow showed him a ship in a bottle that floated like a ship inside of a larger bottle that was blown into the shape of a ship and that had an inscription pasted to its side which read, "Your time will come." Meir didn't like that either. There was a life-sized stone statue of an eagle grappling with a python, a potato that had grown in the shape of a one-legged quail with no head, and a model of the Leaning Tower of Pisa that was made entirely out of crow bones and kept falling over. Nothing seemed quite right to the shoemaker.

Having refused them all, Meir left the shopkeepers and sat down in the street to think. A group of boys were just coming out of a nearby schoolhouse. On the head of one of the lads was an exquisite yarmulke of white satin, intricately embroidered with a fine, golden thread that glistened in the sunlight. Dazzled, the shoemaker watched the boy sit himself on the schoolhouse steps where he unwrapped a filet of pickled herring and started to eat.

"Little boy!" called Meir, rushing toward the lad who looked up in surprise and covered his herring with both hands.

"Hello there," Meir went on, smiling and winking and taking a seat alongside the boy.

The lad, scrutinizing the interloper, rewrapped the herring and slid it behind his back.

"What's your name?" asked Meir.

The boy remained silent.

"That's one fine yarmulke you have on. I wish I had one like it. Oh, look! It has gotten a bit old, hasn't it?"

"It's brand new! I only got it three weeks ago for my Bar Mitzvah!"

"And already so worn out. It's practically coming apart. What a shame. So much for craftsmanship these days."

"It can't be," said the boy, taking the cap off of his head to examine it.

"But it is! Take my word for it. You need a trained eye. It won't last," said Meir, putting an arm around the lad's shoulders. "This is a lucky day for you. I happen to be a collector of old yarmulkes. It's a hobby. People tell me I throw my money away on the things, but what can you do? I enjoy it. And when you're as rich as I am, what else can you do with your money? For instance, I'd give you six kopeks for that rag of yours. Crazy, right? The thing is ready to come apart, but there you have it. That's what I'm like. You could buy two new ones with that money and still have a little left over for a nice sugar-roll."

Looking from the shoemaker to the yarmulke and back at the shoemaker again, the boy began to cry.

"Now, now," said Meir, glancing around to make sure that no one was watching. "Is that a way for a bar mitzvah boy to act...Hello...Can you hear me? Shhh, shah, now shah...All right, you strike a hard bargain, but I like you and I hate to see someone in such sorrow. I'll give you a whole ruble!"

Holding his tears, the lad touched the shiny coin that Meir proffered and a soft radiance came over his face. Then he resumed his caterwauling, more tearfully than ever, loud enough to attract attention.

"Enough!" hollered the shoemaker, emptying his pockets. "Here! Take it all! Just shut up and give me that yarmulke!"

The boy snatched the money, threw the hat into Meir's face, and ran off without his herring. Relieved, the shoemaker stared at the yarmulke, twirling it on a finger. He would have remained there for the rest of the day, captivated by the way daylight played on the surface of the little cap, had not a scavenging feline sneaked up from behind the schoolhouse and pounced on the boy's forgotten fish with a hair-raising screech. The startled shoemaker jumped to his feet and, before he came to his senses, was off to the Besht's.

Though it took a while to find it, Meir knew Israel's house as soon as he saw it. There was no mistaking it. It was orange. The front, the sides, the roof; all orange. The window curtains were orange and the mat that the shoemaker stepped onto, in front of the orange door, was orange.

Meir ran his hands along his clothes to smooth the creases, and combed his hair with his fingers. He was about to knock when the door opened.

"Yes, I'm sorry, we're not receiving visitors today," said a very bent and elderly woman.

"But I'm here to see the Besht."

"Well, there are four or five Beshts on this street alone; why don't you try one of the others?"

"No. This has got to be the right house. He's expecting me."

"You're too late, Ship-maker," said a young man who came up alongside of the old woman. It was the same fellow whom Meir had met earlier.

"I'm awfully sorry I'm late, but..."

"No, I'm sorry. The Besht is dead."

"Dead? It can't be. Only this morning..."

"That was this morning."

"It's not possible."

"It's more than possible."

"How?"

"He was ill and he died. It happened a little while ago."

"He can't be! Are you sure? Have another look!"

"Please, there are things to take care of," said the man, closing the door.

Meir didn't know what to do or where to turn. Calling for Israel, he banged and kicked at the orange door. No one answered anymore. At last, he gave up and walked away.

On the outskirts of Medzhibozh, Meir seated himself beneath the bowers of a willow, his back against its furrowed bark. Losing his friend, and hoped-for teacher, had formed a tight knot of grief in his chest. It lodged there, hard as a walnut, pressing against his heart, making every breath difficult.

"That clown, Luckshinkopf, was right," he

thought. "I never should have left Warsaw. Uncle Mottle tried to stop me, but would I listen? I had to go off and trade everything, a decent life, for God knows what. Only Rachel agreed with me that it was a good idea. What does she know? She's almost as young as I am. And now it's all a mess. A year to go from there to here, and I'm still nowhere, a nothing, nobody but a cobbler. I wish I were the one who was dead.

"That's what dreams are like," continued Meir aloud. "They promise a lot, so you put everything into them until they get as big as monsters. Then they squash you."

"The same as a woman," responded a voice.

"Who said that?" called Meir and when no one answered after a good while, he shook his head. "It's not enough that my life stinks, I have to go crazy, too! I should just sit here until I sink into the earth. Maybe one of these trees will suck me up and I'll come out in a nice, cool, green leaf. Nobody cares if a leaf goes crazy."

"Relax. All I said was that you can describe a woman the same way as you described dreams," said the voice, but as Meir looked up this time, he saw old Israel coming toward him. "You find one that you can't get your mind off of and pretty soon she's got a finger in each of your nostrils, pulling you every which way. You pour your life into her and she gets bigger and bigger. One day, she hops into bed on top of you and...crunch!"

The shoemaker's face turned the color of sour cream. His head twitched to one side and a stiffening chill ran up his back. Both of his knees collapsed toward each other, meeting with a loud knock.

"You're too tense," said Israel. "It's not healthy."

"You're dead!"

"So? It offends you? You don't look so well either."

When Meir tried to speak again, he couldn't. Clicking sounds came from the back of his throat. A puddle widened at his feet, from a trickle that came from the sleeves of his trousers.

"Now look what you've done!" Israel scolded. "Disgusting! I'm not saying another word to you until you get a hold on yourself!"

The two men stood and looked at each other; Meir trembling in his wet shoes, Israel with folded arms, shifting his weight from one leg to the other, chewing the corners of his moustache. Ten, fifteen, twenty minutes passed and the bored, old man started to hum. Meir, looking on as the apparent ghost called up a confusing medley of liturgical chants, melancholy airs, and raucous folk songs in dubious keys, felt silly. He forgot to keep shaking.

His heart stopped thumping and though he tried to pump it up by breathing heavily, it was a lost cause. He simply wasn't afraid any longer and, with the old man getting ready to run through his repertoire for the third time, Meir realized that he would have to say something or stand there forever, feeling more and more ridiculous.

"Nice tunes," he offered feebly.

"He speaks! Blessed is God's name! Now maybe we can get down to business. We've got to hurry. There are things to do and I'm under a lot of pressure."

"Pressure?"

"You bet! What do you think; it's easy being dead? Forget it! I've had to get used to a completely different way of life. It's affected my appetite, thrown my whole system off. Why, I haven't had a bite since my last breath, and look! I'm gaining weight!"

Lifting his arms up and turning sideways, Israel displayed his newly revived paunch to Meir. All signs of the old man's illness were gone. His cheeks glowed with the same ruddy good health that they had when the two friends first met.

"I should be dropping pounds with all my worries," the old fellow went on, "but I'm putting it on by the shovelful!"

"You look great! What troubles can you have?"

"What can I have? Go back to thinking you're crazy; you were right! How do I know what I'll find in heaven? Maybe just people standing around and singing all the time with worse voices than mine! And you've seen how fat most women get before they die! I don't hold it against them; I like big women. But when they get all lumpy, it gives me headaches! What if they're all like that up there! With wings and those flimsy nightgowns that don't hide anything! It could be a catastrophe!"

"You're not serious..."

"Serious-shmerious, this is death! What if the Christians have been right all along? Or the Moslems? Imagine my embarrassment! Sure, I've spoken to God about it, but he's not talking. You know how tricky he can be. It would be just like him to not exist when I get there. Just for spite! And do you have any idea how many people have died since the beginning of time? What if I can't find a room?"

"You're the Baal Shem Tov; surely..."

"Baal Shem Tov! Master of the Good Name! Big deal! Do you know where the word "Baal" comes from? A stone idol that couldn't even scratch its own nose if it wanted to! Look it up! Tell a few stories, dance a little prayer, talk to a bird or two, and what happens? They give you a title! Then they follow you around like a pack of hungry cats and you're a saucer of milk! You've got to bless their businesses, find jobs for their children, and heaven forbid a woman should be barren! They don't know whether to eat with the spoon in the right hand or the left, unless you tell them! And what do you get for your trouble? Other people die and, bing-bang-boom, they're in heaven, rubbing elbows with famous personalities, maybe munching a bit of fruitcake with King David himself! But you, Mr. Baal Shem Tov? What happens when you die? Clerical work!"

Meir pinched himself. When he didn't wake up, he wondered whether he really had lost his mind.

"Which brings me to what I wanted to talk to you about," continued Israel as he dragged a large sack out from behind some nearby shrubbery and dumped enough papers out of it to form a sizable hill at the shoemaker's feet. "These are all prayers and hopes and things that I promised folks I'd take to heaven for them so they shouldn't get lost. We've got to organize them. You know, urgent prayers with urgent prayers, good deeds with good deeds, and so on, and then alphabetize the lot by name."

At that instant, several dozen of the larger sheets of paper floated up into the air and fluttered over the treetops. Meir tried to catch some of them before they got away.

"Don't worry about those," said the Besht. "I only

took them down, in the first place, to get some people off of my back. They're just accusations. Seems like a lot, but very little substance. Just tell me you'll help me."

"I don't feel very..."

"Good! And when we're finished, I'll give you that blessing and we can be off, each to his particular heaven. Rachel was her name, wasn't it? I'll even provide the transportation."

Without wasting another moment, the two companions got a fire going and attacked the massive stack of paper with all four hands.

"What are these?" asked Meir, holding up a number of blank sheets.

"Oh, you can throw those away. Those are lists of ambitions. People insist on telling them to me. I write them down with vanishing ink."

"That's awful!"

"Where's your sense of humor!"

"And what about this list here? It's marked 'achievements,' but it only has one item on it: Simchik, son of Reb Yankle the schoolmaster, remained in the air for two and one half minutes before he smashed into the side of a flour-mill and broke all of his bones."

"You should have seen him. Very impressive."

"It's the only thing on the list!"

"It's the only real achievement I ever saw."

"A person killed himself!"

"He only crippled himself. And he's a very happy cripple, I might add. Quite a fellow! What a sight! The way he soared from one side of the street to the other! Ever since he was a boy, he wanted to fly like that. He was made for it too. A build like a flatworm, but with arms so strong that he could flap them all day long. Whenever you saw him, he was flapping. And not a word of support from anyone. His own father, after years of pleading and threatening, countless beatings with leather straps and cooking pots, couldn't get this Simchik to give it up. Just flap, flap, flap, all the time.

"Then, one afternoon about three days before Passover, people heard laughter over their heads, looked up, and there he was. It didn't last long, but they all had to hand it to him. Even his cranky, old father had to give in and congratulate his son. So two legs had to be removed. They built some wheels into a board, sat him on it, and he learned to push himself around with those strong arms of his. Whatever you may think about it, Simchik always had a smile on his face after that, and the townsfolk treated him with utmost respect."

"That's not an achievement; it's a horror story!"

"Jealous?"

"Why isn't there anything else on your list? People are doing things all the time."

"If there's one thing that death teaches you, it's that getting somewhere is not the same thing as an achievement. For instance, say there's an idiot, a total loon, and this fellow has terrible skin with all types of pimples and eruptions. He happens to be out in the woods one day, grazing like a sheep, and he gobbles down some plant, without knowing what it is, and it clears up his skin. Just like that; bing-bang-boom and clear.

"It also happens that many of the other people in his village suffer the same skin problems. When the idiot returns home, they all see his lovely, smooth complexion. They're amazed. Surrounding the poor dolt, they ply him with questions. But he's as much in the dark as they are. Still, they badger the fellow so much that his head spins, his stomach grumbles, and up comes a mouthful of grass. Now these people are no fools. They can put two and two together. In no time at all, they're all out in the woods, grazing like sheep themselves. Wouldn't you guess, Shipmaker, it's bing-bang-boom for them too. By the next day, there's not a pimple in town. A miracle! A marvelous discovery! But is it an achievement? The dolt didn't do anything but get hungry and fill his belly."

"All right, I get your point," said Meir.

"No, there's more. As you can imagine, this idiot becomes a very popular fellow. Everybody loves him and thinks he's one smart old fox. In fact, they can hardly believe how well and how humbly he had kept his wisdom hidden from them. They name a street after him, and throw a big banquet in his honor where he is elected to preside over the village council of elders.

"Once elected, the new President declares every odd numbered day and half of the even numbered days of the week to be feast days. All of the women are put to work making puddings of dry grass. The men are ordered to sit in buckets and give a quart of milk each day for the festivities. If they fail, they're fined seventy-five percent of their children. Youngsters collected in this way are made to decorate the streets with garlands of flowers so that the President can ride over the buds in a wheelbarrow pulled by the other members of the council.

"That's an achievement! Not the lucky accident that they gave him credit for, but when the idiot has taken his own special talent and raised it to a higher level, infecting a whole town! When a person does something like that, he fulfills his own best destiny in such a way that applause is drawn from the angels and his name is inscribed on the surface of the moon!"

"Uh huh," said Meir, wondering who was the biggest idiot; the dolt in the story, the old man for telling it, or himself for sitting there, going through papers with the ghost of a holy man whose fables were just as preposterous dead as when he was alive.

Meir was sure of only one thing; grief had cracked his mind and he was now utterly mad. The certainty of it provided him a high degree of relief. It didn't trouble him at all, because it didn't matter. His brain could turn to compote, leaving him as witless as a pigeon, and he would be no worse off than most everyone else in the world. The earth was loaded with lunatics. The heavens as well, for all he knew. God Himself might be the craziest, cackling loon there was. That was a thought, mused Meir, that knocked the doors off their hinges.

The ghost and the shoemaker continued to work alongside of each other until the night had passed and the sun rose like a taut, red bubble above the trees. Then, folding a final handful of papers and dropping them into the sack, Israel announced that they had finished. Meir breathed a deep sigh and gave a good stretch to his limbs.

"And now the blessing!" proclaimed the old man.

"Let it wait until after we get some sleep," yawned the shoemaker.

"No time for that. Now or forget it."

"Wait, I almost did forget something."

Fumbling in his pockets, Meir eventually produced the white satin yarmulke that he had purchased in Medzhibozh.

"It's a gift," he said.

"Very nice," replied Israel, taking the cap and turning it over in his hands. "But a little flashy for where I'm going. I want to make a good impression. You'd better keep it."

Too tired to be much disappointed, Meir stuffed the hat back into his trousers and stood waiting for the blessing.

"Good health!" pronounced the ghost.

"That's it, good health?"

"You want more? Hmmm...I have it! My blessing on that hat!"

"That's not funny! I need something firmer than that! How about something definite! Some direction!"

"Don't be so cranky. I can't help it if you're hard to please today. This is my last try. I think I have a good one now. Ready?"

"Ready."

"May every shoe find the proper foot!"

"Shoes! That's not..." began the shoemaker, cutting himself short with a violent sneeze that pushed his head back and forced his eyes to shut. When he opened them again, Israel and the sack of papers were gone.

"No you don't!" yelled Meir, brandishing his fist. "You don't go pulling this vanishing stuff again! Some blessing! Who needs it?! You could have at least loaned me a couple of kopeks! How am I going to get home? You promised transportation!"

Meir screamed until his throat was sore and he was too weary to continue. Leaning against the willow, he slid to the ground, falling asleep in an instant. After a moment or so, his eyes snapped back open. A sparrow had landed on his shoulder and was pecking at his ear.

"Wake and shake," chirped the little bird between pecks. "Wake and shake. Wake and shake."

Then the entire area darkened with moving shadows. Leaves rustled furiously as the branches of trees creaked with sudden weight. Hundreds of tiny eyes peered out of the bowers. Getting to his feet and waving his arms around, the shoemaker couldn't drive off the sparrow that continued to flutter about his head.

"Wake and shake, wake and shake," it repeated.

Eagles, land rails, starlings, rooks, and robins descended like a net of fantastic plumage. Doves flew wing to wing with hawks, owls, jackdaws, and larks.

Magpies swooshed down, screeching as they came. Cuckoos spun in eccentric circles, adding their eerie squeals to the whistles of the bullfinches, the honking of flocks of geese, and the twitterings of nightingales. Touching ground, the birds merged into a carpet of feathers that unrolled across the field and gathered around Meir's feet. The shoemaker, losing his balance as the downy blanket lifted, fell into the warm, waving folds beneath him. Loosed feathers twirled in the air. By the time that Meir regained a clear view of things, there was nothing for him to see but the endless blue of the sky and wispy clouds that whisked by with dizzying speed.

"Am I dead?" begged the shoemaker. "I don't want to be dead!" Then the feathery carpet made a wide, tilting turn and Meir caught sight of the vast plain of Poland below, falling further and further out of reach. Grabbing on with both hands, Meir plunged his nose into the undulating mesh of wings and braced himself for he didn't know what.

10 &

MEIR WAS BAFFLED. ONE MOMENT HE WAS
soaring through space, borne aloft by a nightmarish
mass of birds; the next he lay in a crooked heap where
he had to locate and untangle his limbs before he
could move them well enough to raise himself to an
upright position. His mouth was full of dirt. When
he blew his nose, feathers flew out of it. Shaking
his head to clear his senses, the wobbling shoemaker
could hardly believe his eyes as he found himself
looking out over the Vistula toward Warsaw and
home.

Without an eye's blink worth of hesitation, Meir
dashed across the bridge that led to the entrance of
the city. Soon his feet were touching the familiar
streets and he felt like dancing. In deep breaths, he
took in the smells of fresh baking and horse manure.
Crowing roosters and the clanging bells of peddlers'
carts drew him to the market where grey-bearded
Jews argued with feather-capped peasants in jodhpurs
and embroidered waistcoats over the price of skins.
Lusty farm-girls carried bowls of fruit and linen-

covered baskets, widely swaying their broad hips as they made their ways through the mud and crowds. One stout woman bathed her daughter at a well, dumping bucketfuls of icy water on the fidgeting child who shivered and slapped her hands against her own belly. Sagging horses stood in rows before overloaded carts of vegetables and fleece. Students walked arm in arm, coattails wagging, mouths moving in spirited conversations that were lost in the jumbled din and rumble that were Warsaw at midday.

Remembering Israel, Meir blessed the old man with every blessing that he could think of, throwing in the benediction for wine and the one for Hanukkah lights when all the more appropriate blessings were exhausted. The old fellow had kept his word and provided the transportation that delivered the shoemaker home. Meir pledged never to forget the favor. After he married Rachel, all of their sons would be named Israel. Meir swore he would someday make a pair of shoes to honor the old man, a pair that were really something special, a devout pair; shoes that would refuse to walk on the Sabbath! Why not? What could stop him? That he, Meir, was an expert with shoes no one had ever doubted. Now that he was home, he was ready to get down to business. If the shoes that he made did have a tendency to take on a life of their own, he would learn to control them.

After all, he made the shoes and not the other way around. He had the authority. Maybe he would use it to make the most magnificent bit of cobblery ever to be seen.

Thrilled as he was by all of the possibilities that his homecoming presented to him, Meir put these ambitions aside. At present, he wanted nothing better than to put his arms around his Uncle Mottle. So, with a rush of youthful energy, the shoemaker hoisted his sack and set off at a trot.

"Meir!" cheered Mottle when he answered the knocking at his door to find his nephew waiting for him with a big hug.

"Uncle!" Meir responded.

"My boy, my lovely boy! Glückel, set out some cheese dumplings! My nephew's home! Look for that chicken I've been fattening up!"

"Who is this Glückel you're calling?"

"My new wife! You'll love her! What a cook she is! But come in, my boy. Don't stand outside when a house is hungry for you," said the uncle, taking Meir's hands in his own and pulling the younger man inside.

"Did you say wife?"

"That's what I said. What else should I call her? That's what she is. You missed it. What a romance we had! I wouldn't believe my good fortune if I didn't know she was in the yard right now, chasing down that chicken. And wait till you see that bird! So plump, you can't find its feet!"

"So this is Meir," said a pleasant-looking woman who came up alongside Uncle Mottle. She was short, even next to Mottle, with a generous smile and pink cheeks that seemed all the pinker because of a sparse, white down that grew on her upper lip. The chicken that she held by the neck was every bit as plump as Mottle had promised, but no plumper than the new wife or, for that matter, Uncle Mottle himself.

"I'm very glad to meet you," said Meir.

"Mottle has told me all about you. He's been very worried. Come, I'll make you a nice meal, we'll sit, talk, and you can have a good rest. Everything's going to be better now."

"Has anything been wrong?"

"Not now," Mottle cut in. "First, we'll eat. You must have some stories to tell. A whole year! Did you ever find that Besht fellow? Glückel, my pancake, that chicken is crying for the pot."

"Let it keep for a while, Uncle," said Meir, starting out the door. "I've got to go see Rachel to tell her I'm back and that we can get married right away."

"You just got home!"

"I'm sorry, I won't be long."

"But wait!" shouted the uncle. It was too late.

Meir was already halfway down the street and well out of earshot.

"Don't get excited," soothed Glückel. "You know what happens when you get excited."

"Boy oh boy, the poor lad. It's terrible, just terrible."

"Ahhchoo!" Mottle released a savage sneeze and Glückel, dropping the bird, ran for her life.

Arriving at Rabbi Zaydle's house, Meir was so stirred up that he bruised his knuckles hammering on the door. A wooden panel slid open and two, heavily lidded eyes, set on a queer tilt, peered out at him. The panel shut, opened again, and the eyes blinked three times.

"What do you want?" asked the rabbi's wife.

"It's Meir the shoemaker. I'd like to see Rachel."

The panel closed again and Meir listened to the scraping of the woman's feet as it faded into the house and was replaced by the firmer, more determined steps of her approaching husband. This time, when the panel opened, it was two sharp, whiskered cheekbones that Meir faced.

"Too late!" announced the rabbi.

"Too late?"

"She's taken! What do you think, that I'm going to sit on a catch like Rachel while you go off to witch doctors?"

"We were matched!"

"Canceled! By default! There's been a better offer!"

"You can't..."

"Done!"

"I want to talk to..."

"Talk to a wall! She'll be married in three weeks! To a winner! A butcher's son! And I get all the meat I want at discount! How's that for a generous boy? You know him; Ezer! Why don't you go talk to him?" and the rabbi slammed the panel.

Meir did know Ezer. In fact, he knew him well enough to know that the bullying son of a butcher was not a fellow that could be reasoned with. Head bent, the shoemaker headed for home.

Back at the house, Glückel met Meir as he was coming in. She was out of breath. Both of her eyes were black and her dress was torn.

"My God, what happened to you?" asked Meir.

"He got me good this time. But he's asleep now."

"Who? Uncle Mottle? He did this?"

"Not really. In one sense, he...but it wasn't him."

"Then who?"

"The first wife, Flanka!"

"But she's dead."

"I used to think that Mottle had lost his mind.

Now I don't know anymore. He claims it's your aunt," said Glückel, beginning to cry.

"Tell me how it happened," said Meir as he put his arms around the woman. "We're family. You can tell me."

"It starts with a sneeze, always with a sneeze. We were so happy, a widow and a widower, both lonely. It was a nice match. I cooked and he ate. It made me tingle all over, excuse me, just to watch him."

"So what went wrong?" Meir asked, though he was only half listening. His mind kept drifting back to Rachel and Ezer.

"We got married."

"And that's wonder..."

"And everything changed! On our wedding night ...the first time we...he sneezed!"

"There's nothing so terrible about that. Many men do it. It's a sign of sensitivity."

"It is terrible! He keeps doing it! Whenever he's excited, he sneezes! And when he does...Flanka!"

"What are you saying?"

"A transformation! He becomes Flanka! He still looks like himself, but he's her. Her manner! Her mind! Her voice! It's awful! The first time that it happened, she chased me around the house with a broom, screaming 'Harlot!' out of your uncle's mouth as she came, 'Husband stealer! Petty thief!'

Terrifying! That shrill voice! Who knew what was happening? I ran over the furniture, tossing chairs behind me while that broom swooshed at my head!"

"My God!"

"She trapped me in the kitchen. I pulled the cover off of a pot of cabbage that I had cooking, meaning to use it to fend her off, but Mottle's nose started to twitch at the aroma of the sweet and sour sauce and he was suddenly himself again. My cabbage was always his favorite. We wept in each other's arms."

"And this transformation has taken place again?"

"And again and again and again! We can't stop it! Sometimes he sits, clamping his nose between two fingers, but it doesn't help. Sooner or later, he sneezes and I'm in trouble. I'm going mad! You've got to think of something!"

Giving her hand a squeeze, Meir promised his aunt that he wouldn't rest until he came up with a solution to her and Mottle's problem.

"In the meantime," he said, taking leave of the woman, "you keep that cabbage cooking and make sure that Uncle Mottle stays where he can smell it."

Going over to his old workplace to think, Meir found it exactly as he had left it before going off on his journey to find the Besht. Down to the leather strips and bent nails that littered the floor around his bench, the entire area had been preserved untouched.

This loving consideration of his Uncle's made the young shoemaker more determined to do something to alleviate the good fellow's plight. And yet, despite the best of intentions, it wasn't long before Meir forgot about his relative's troubles and turned to his own. There wasn't room in his mind for any thought that didn't have to do with Rachel.

"It's you!" exclaimed Luckshinkopf in his flute-like voice as he poked his head through the window and stared at the shoemaker. "I knew it! I saw you, and there you were! Like magic! And I wasn't even thinking of you! I was wondering if we only think that the direction that our eyes are looking in is forward because our eyes are looking that way. Now that you're here, I can ask you. Are you ever coming back?"

"No," said Meir darkly.

"Me either."

"Leave me alone."

"Got an apple?"

"Go away!"

"All right, I'll stay," said the fool, scampering away.

Over the next few days, Meir came up with no better plan for getting hold of Rachel than to throw rocks at her window. The rocks came shooting back, hard and fast. The rabbi had taken the precaution of moving into Rachel's room himself and locking the girl away in some other part of the house. When Meir realized the ploy, he took to tossing his stones at every window indiscriminately. To this, the rabbi responded by inviting Ezer to move in until the wedding. The shoemaker was stumped. Surrender seemed his only choice, but he couldn't bring himself to accept it. Turning to his trade to work off his anxiety, Meir exercised his craft with more fervor than ever before.

If some of Meir's shoes had exhibited unique characteristics in the past, they were nothing compared to the ways that they sometimes acted now. People would bring him a perfectly normal pair of shoes which, when returned to them, would turn only to the left, bump into or walk away from one another, or be guilty of some other such unbecoming behavior. The shoemaker, as well as his customers, was often chagrined. There was no way that he could predict what a particular pair might do. People whispered. Rumors circulated about the possible influence of supernatural powers. Still, the undeniable skill of the shoemaker's hands, the superior quality and beauty of his work, assured him a steady flow of patronage.

Meir worked more and more furiously, time hissing in his ears as the days went by. Sharpening tools that didn't need sharpening, mixing and remixing dyes until they turned muddy and grey, taking shoes apart just to put them back together again, he tried everything to get Rachel out of his head and it was all useless. He thought about her. When he thought about her, he pictured her, and when he pictured her, she was looking back at him with a longing that matched his own.

Meanwhile, Glückel had her hands full with Mottle. Meir had been no help to her at all. On the contrary, he had made things worse. The way that the young man was ignoring his elder relations depressed Mottle, and depression aggravated the uncle's condition. Though Glückel continually had some cabbage steaming over a fire, Mottle paced in and out of range of the aroma's beneficial influence. If he was far enough away when he sneezed, Flanka would take over his body and hold it, flinging knives at the new wife, hurling bric-a-brac, threatening to give Glückel's address out to horrendous demons unless she moved out of her, the first wife's, house. Glückel always incurred a number of wounds before she could lure her tormentor into the kitchen where, thanks to the cabbage, Mottle would become Mottle again.

The situation continued to deteriorate. Glückel

was finding it ever more difficult to draw Flanka into the kitchen. The devilish possessor of Mottle's mind clung to her victim with a tenacity that aimed for permanence. Soon nothing would dislodge her. Driven to desperation, Glückel developed a plan.

One night, while Mottle was Mottle, Glückel roused him from his sleep and led him out to the yard where she bound him, head to toe, to a pole. Seven huge tubs of bubbling cabbage were set in a circle around him, thickening the air with the pungent vapor that rose from an especially potent brew. Glückel's three sisters were on hand to keep the pots full and cooking. Though they did as they were asked to do, all three of them grew frightened when Glückel hugged herself to her husband and vowed not to let go until he was cured.

"You must stop this," reasoned the eldest sister. "Just think of all the food you're wasting."

"Give it away," replied Glückel. "But make sure that you put back as much as you take out."

"Who's going to pay for it all?" moaned the youngest sister.

"Sell the furniture, my clothes, anything that you can take out of the house."

"It's so foolish!" insisted the middle sister, stamping her foot. "It won't work, this looking for miracles!"

192 ~

"It will work," said Glückel. "It has to."

It did work. The hungrier that Mottle got, the easier it was for him to fight his first wife back. After a sneeze, Flanka barely had time for a single shriek before Mottle's stomach growled and the good fellow, following the edge of his appetite back to a cabbage-scented reality, wrested control of his own mind for himself.

From time to time, both Mottle and Glückel called to Meir but he didn't hear them. Neither did he pay any attention to the chatter of Glückel's sisters when they brought him plates of cabbage to pick at as he worked. Day after day, with Rachel's wedding approaching, the young shoemaker remained unaware of his relatives' long embrace behind the house, of how the moisture from the steaming cabbage made them stick together, and of how the cold, dry night air cracked and hardened their skin and clothes into bark. So deep was Meir's brood that the weeping of Glückel's sisters failed to penetrate it when, from staying in one position for so long, Mottle's and Glückel's toenails lengthened and burrowed into the earth, and thin, leafy branches sprouted from their ears.

It wasn't until the day before Rachel was to be married that Meir woke up to the world again. He got an idea. It blossomed before him, part rose and part sun, and breathless he snatched it. It was so obvious that he wondered why he had taken so long to see it. It must have been there, right under his nose, all along. All that he needed to do was to make a pair of shoes that would follow orders. They were always acting up anyway. Now was the time to assert his authority and take control. He would get these shoes to leap so high and jump so far that he would be able to pounce on the wedding party and bound off with Rachel before anyone knew what hit them.

Intoxicated with the plot, Meir immediately began to cut and fit pieces of leather. As he worked, he concentrated his will on the shoes forming under his hands.

"Jump…Jump…Jump," he repeated, as if the words could burn themselves into the leather.

For the first time since he was turned away from the rabbi's door, Meir forgot about Rachel. The only picture that was in his mind now was of himself making the triumphant leap over the heads of an awed crowd. He saw the rabbi turning angry shades of purple and red, Ezer running through the streets and begging for mercy, dozens of hands clapping themselves raw. No longer just "the shoemaker," Meir would be "the acrobat," the greatest acrobat in all Poland. People would swarm in from the countryside to see him jump and to wager on how many minutes he could remain aloft. Minutes? Hours! He would tap his knuckles on the roof of the world and push up the floorboards of heaven.

"After tomorrow," said the shoemaker to his handiwork, "they'll know the kind of man I am. We'll be famous. Maybe rich!"

The shoes were ready that evening, with plenty of time to spare, but Meir refused to sleep. He was afraid that any lapse of concentration might cost him his success. Head aching, eyes bloodshot and burning, he persisted in pressing his desire into the footwear.

"Jump... Jump... Jump," he continued with purpose.

When morning came, Meir was waiting for it. Nearly delirious with expectation, he arrived at the rabbi's house as the ceremony was about to begin and stood outside the yard, behind the fence so he wouldn't be seen. Through the slats of the fence Meir, rubbing his hands together, saw Ezer's wide back looming over the other people like the side of a cliff. Next to Ezer, fragile by comparison and all in white, was Rachel. Her hair had been clipped so short that not a strand showed from under her kerchief to lend color to her pale face. Yet, the shoemaker was stunned by how lovely she looked. He felt ashamed that he had allowed himself to forget her for even a second.

The rabbi took his place, went through the preliminary benedictions, and filled a glass with the wine that would be used to consecrate the marriage. Kicking off the shoes that he was wearing, Meir attempted to slip into the new ones. They gave him a hard time. He pushed in one foot after the other only to have them each pop out again in turn.

"Behold you are made holy unto me..." Ezer spoke his prescribed portion in tones as slow and deep as the low of a cow, while the sweating shoemaker fumbled and tripped over his own feet, "... according to the laws of Moses and Israel."

Then, when Rachel bent her head to sip the wine from the glass offered her by the rabbi, Meir managed at last to squeeze both feet into the shoes at once and stand in them before they could fly off. Bending his knees, reaching his arms back as far as they would go, he threw himself upward with all of the strength that was in him. Every bone in his body crackled. His knees snapped and his arms dislocated from his shoulders, freezing in place. With a long moan, the shoemaker stepped out of the immovable shoes, stumbled along the fence, and slid to the ground from where he heard the sound of the wine glasses being smashed by a large foot, announcing the completion of the ceremony.

When the festivities were over, few of the departing guests took notice of the crumpled shoemaker. Rachel stopped for a moment, but Ezer quickly caught up with her and whisked her into his arms, laughing as he tucked her up. Meir, barefoot and leg-twisted, his paralyzed arms extended above his head, stretched his neck painfully and saw Rachel glancing back at him from over the shoulder of the husband who held her tightly and carried her away.

"Nice day," said Luckshinkopf, tripping over out of nowhere and bending down so close to Meir's face that their noses almost touched. "Looks like rain."

In several months, Meir was well enough to be trundling about the city with his cart again. As well as owing a good deal of money for his own medical expenses, the shoemaker was in debt to the grocer and the butcher for the phenomenal amounts of cabbage and chopped meat that had gone to Uncle Mottle's cure. And though Uncle Mottle *was* cured, the amelioration of his fiendish sneezing had left the good fellow in a state that was not conducive to the earning of any money for himself. He and Glückel were now a tree that stood in the yard. As such, they were not even good company for Meir. Short and thick, their trunk a convergence of sturdy roots that wound around each other, they remained quite silent.

Only the sweet and sour smell that was on their white, bell-shaped blossoms resembled anything that might masquerade as a communication.

So, seeking work as hard as he could, Meir rang his bell and peddled his services up and down Warsaw's streets. Now and again, as chance would have it, he and Rachel crossed paths. On these occasions, they lowered their heads and passed one another without a word in greeting. Still, when he was sure that she wouldn't notice, the young shoemaker followed Ezer's wife out of the corners of his eyes.

Ezer, on the other hand, never met up with Meir without stopping to have some fun.

"Don't know why she needs shoes in the first place," the butcher's son once said, handing Meir a pair of Rachel's slippers. "I try to keep her off her feet; know what I mean, shoemaker? Have you seen the bruises I've had to give her? That's because she's such a tigress, can't get enough of me. You're lucky; she'd have killed you. But me, I know how to handle her."

Ezer enjoyed Meir's companionship so much that he became the shoemaker's most faithful and fastidious customer. If he didn't have shoes of his own that needed fixing, he borrowed broken ones from someone else. And if Meir didn't repair them exactly the way that he wanted them, Ezer kept the money and paid with a kick instead. The brute was rarely pleased.

One week after his father died and he inherited the business, Ezer brought his favorite work-boots to Meir for a cleaning. While the shoemaker scrubbed at the grease and blood, Ezer stood by menacingly, kneading the palm of one hand with the mallet-like fist of the other, meanness gleaming hopefully in his eyes. But this time, when Meir handed him the shoes, the butcher couldn't find anything to complain about. The boots looked better than the day he had bought them. Gritting his teeth, Ezer put on the boots, pushed fifty kopeks into Meir's hand, and stormed off.

Almost at once, the shoes began to walk on their toes. Some force lifted them against Ezer's mighty effort and, to his astonishment, they began to skip, pirouette, and twirl. The butcher had to hold his arms out to his sides to keep balanced. Meir had never seen anything like it. Ezer, frolicking compulsively, hands waving loosely on his outstretched arms, roared curses that drowned in the horse-laughs of passers-by.

Charging out of the gathering crowd, holding her dress up above her knees as she came, Rachel chased after the spinning Goliath and tried to take hold of him.

"Don't get so close!" warned Meir, grabbing the distraught woman by the wrist and pulling her away. "You could get trampled!"

"I've got to do something!" she replied, tugging at her arm while Ezer bounded out of town with a series of high revolving leaps.

"Let him go."

"He's my husband!"

"Can't you tell a miracle when you see one? We're a match!"

"You're crazy!"

"We'll get out of Warsaw! Who likes it here anyway!"

"Let me go!"

"It's too late," said Meir, pointing toward where Ezer's figure had already faded in the direction of Praga forest. "What if he never comes back?"

"I'd still be his wife!" shouted Rachel as she finally pulled free of the shoemaker and backed away from him. "It's the law! I can't get a divorce without him!"

But Ezer did come back. After a night of bouncing about the forest, his head banging on countless branches, the boots simply fell from his feet. He was rankled. When he found Meir, the butcher lifted the shoemaker's cart and smashed it to the ground. Meir barely got away without falling into the fellow's murderous clutches himself. Rachel didn't fare so well. Cornering her at home, Ezer pulled a fistful of hair out of her head for not catching him.

Meir's business suffered from the incident. People were afraid to let him near their shoes lest the same thing happen to them that happened to the butcher. Only those with the oddest senses of humor used him, mostly buying shoes for other people. The practice became a common joke.

Lonely as he was, with only the Mottle-Glückel tree to talk to, Meir took comfort in burying his nose in his work. The days and weeks meant nothing to him. Months, and then years, were just stacks of nothing that separated, one by one, and scattered on the wind like white sheets of paper. He still thought of Rachel, and these thoughts were precious, secret things that he kept hidden in his heart. They, and the beautifully embroidered yarmulke that he had saved from his time with the Besht, were all that was valuable to him.

11 🦢

MEIR LIVED QUIETLY FOR A VERY LONG TIME, growing a thick, grey beard, having little come into his life to disturb it. He never married. For company, he had the children who occasionally came to listen to the stories he told as he sat, leaning over his work-table, making and mending shoes. Some of the stories were true; some he made up as he went along. It didn't matter. The children believed or disbelieved as they wished and, in either case, Meir got his work done. The bit of money that he earned from thus plying his trade was usually enough for his needs. He rarely went hungry. The holes in the roof did not outnumber his pots and bowls.

Despite the weight of his years, the shoemaker stopped working several times a day to carry himself to the market where he invariably visited Dov Leibish's tannery. Meir enjoyed a good walk. He liked the gentle ache that he felt in his legs and feet after one, and the wooly fatigue that came over him, portending a sound sleep later on. But there was more that brought the shoemaker to the tannery so regularly. For one, there was Luckshinkopf. Meir had a special interest in this fool who had taken up residence inside of a rusty bucket that stood outside of Dov Leibish's shop.

Luckshinkopf had jigged his last long ago. Like anyone else whose life extends beyond a certain number of years, he got old. His legs became as thin as straws, losing all of the spring that they had ever held. While he had been able to gambol and jibe, pleased spectators were glad to toss him a coin or look the other way as he pocketed a pear, a radish, an onion from their tables. But when his back no longer flipped, and his arms were too weak to flap, these same folks remembered the value of money and their rights of property. It got so Luckshinkopf's hands hurt less from their deformity than from the thwacks that they received from vigilant grocers.

No longer entertaining enough to be called a clown, nor amusing enough to be referred to as a fool, Luckshinkopf was renamed "the beggar." That seemed to depress the fellow.

"I'm leaving and never coming back!" he announced one afternoon, as loudly as his feeble lungs would allow, and then promptly planted himself in one of the discarded pails, stinking of tanbark and lye soap, that Dov Leibish left littered about the neighborhood of his tannery.

It was a miserable sight. The fool's arms and legs hung over the bucket's rim like dead fish; his skeletal head, tongue lolling out of it, swayed from side to side on a neck that was barely able to support it. He refused to eat. The neighbors were indignant, and a confused Dov Leibish bore the brunt of their complaints.

"He's an eyesore!" charged Ezer the butcher. "You'd better do something about that beggar if you know what's good for you!"

"You realize, Tanner," began Yitzik-Tushele the advocate, "that the value of everyone's property around here will decline, and you are responsible."

"Buckets for the poor," considered Gonif-Yankle the moneylender, tapping the side of his nose. "There ought to be *some* rent involved."

"He smells," whined Dov Leibish's young wife, Pulke, grimacing. "Who knows what he's doing in that bucket? And those clothes! You can see right through them! It's too disgusting! There's nothing there! Make him go away, Leibishnik."

"I'll pay a fair price for the rest of your buckets," offered Gonif-Yankle.

"We should drop that bucket down a well," Ezer suggested, "the fool with it and the tanner after."

"Don't you love me?" cooed Pulke, pressing up against her husband.

"Once Glemp the magistrate hears about this," continued Yitzik-Tushele, "there is bound to be a new tax to pay."

"Taxes?" cried Gonif-Yankle.

The angry congregation met day after day to voice its protestations. Dov Leibish despaired. He was losing business. His wife wouldn't sleep with him. Only Meir stopped by to check on the condition of the bucketed idiot without throwing threats into the tanner's face.

"You've got to help me," Dov Leibish pleaded with the shoemaker. "He knows you. Since you're both old, maybe he'll listen to you. Get him to go away. Tell him I'll find him a room somewhere."

"Look at the fellow," replied Meir, pointing at Luckshinkopf. "He's starving himself. He doesn't have the strength to get out of that pail if he wanted to."

"Then get him to eat something. Quick, before he dies on me," begged the tanner, pushing an apple into Meir's hands.

"He refuses to eat?"

"Not a nibble in God knows how long. How I've tried!"

Meir shrugged and nodded. Taking the apple, he walked over to the fool.

"How about an apple?" he asked.

"Talk to me on Tuesday," replied Luckshinkopf.

"This is Tuesday."

"Talk to me on Wednesday."

"Just have a bite of this apple, you'll like it."

"That's no apple."

"No? Then what is it?"

"Do you know what an apple is when it's not an apple?"

"What?"

"Do you know what an apple…"

"No, I mean what is it?"

"What's what?"

"An apple when it's not an apple."

"I don't remember. Maybe it's an ox."

"Take the apple."

"You take it."

"I have it, and I'm…"

"You don't!"

"Then what's this?" persisted Meir, holding the apple in front of the fool's eyes.

"Is that an apple?"

"Absolutely!"

"An apple that is an apple, or an apple that isn't?"

"An apple's an apple."

"Moooo."

"Have a bite."

"I have to charm you out of it."

"All right."

"What will I do?"

"Whatever you want."

"I can't do anything."

"Nothing?"

"No."

"Take the apple."

"I know! I can get out of this bucket!"

"Fine. Go ahead."

"You get out of it."

"I'm not in it."

"Moooo."

"Just have one bite."

"It's not an apple."

"It's an apple."

"Moooo."

"Why isn't it an apple?"

"Talk to the bucket," said Luckshinkopf, eyeing the apple warily.

And so it went whenever Meir endeavored to get Luckshinkopf to take some food. Weeks turned into months, the fool getting thinner and thinner, shriveling and shrinking, growing tinier and more bent until he fell entirely into the pail. That was a lucky break for Dov Leibish. Once Luckshinkopf was out of sight, folks ceased to bother about the fellow, and the tanner's life returned to normal.

However, Meir did not give up. He hated that pail and the way the dwindling fool fit better and better within its confines, becoming obscure in the shadow at the bottom of it. Luckshinkopf's resignation reminded him of his own, of how he himself had failed to do the one great thing, without another thought in his head, that the Besht had spoken about. Attempting to save the idiot turned into a devotion, one of the two that the shoemaker practiced at the tannery. The other was watching for Rachel.

Though such a thing was considered to be among the gravest sins, the shoemaker could not keep himself from searching for the butcher's wife in the market crowds. Age had changed her as well, made her plump, wrinkled and spotted her skin. She never returned his gaze. The two had not exchanged a word in more years than Meir could remember.

It wasn't hard for the shoemaker to guess at the misfortunes of Rachel's life. They showed in the tremor of her hands and in the limp that she walked with, the result of many blows delivered to her hip by the fists of her husband, Ezer. Still, Meir looked for her and, when he glimpsed her on the street, he caressed her sagging shoulders within the privacy of his imagination.

"It's not your responsibility," she would say, snuggling into his embrace.

"Then whose? And now I'm bringing you into my sin."

"A sin is a mistake. This is no mistake."

"It's impossible. There's no more substance to this than to a rooster born of a farmer's dream of an egg."

Then Rachel would take Meir by the ears and pull his head toward hers until their lips touched.

A day came when a wealthy Polish merchant from Crakow was passing through Warsaw on business. Dressed in a shirt of yellow satin that was embroidered with velvet, red trousers, and high stockings of white silk, he hurried from stall to stall in the market. Spying Meir and his cart outside of the tannery, where the shoemaker was waving a hunk of cheese over a bucket, the merchant called him over.

"Be a good fellow and resole these for me, won't you?" asked the Pole, holding out an expensive pair of red, high-heeled shoes. "And be quick about it. I have important appointments to keep. Do a good job and I'll double your usual fee. However, if I'm not pleased, I'll beat you."

"Fat purses or meat-cleavers, they're all butchers," thought Meir, the merchant's offer putting him in mind of Ezer's terms of payment.

Turning the shoes over in his hands, the shoemaker inspected the damage by poking his little finger through the holes in the soles.

"These are serious holes," said Meir.

"Well, can you fix them or not?"

"Eight rubles is my *usual* price," offered Meir, quadrupling the actual amount of his regular fee. Eight meant sixteen; a windfall, if the merchant agreed.

"Get to it then! I'm already late!"

Without further ado, Meir went to work with his finest leather and his sharpest, shiniest nails. The movements of his fingers were smooth and precise, making no allowance for error. When he was done, the new soles looked so lovely that it was almost a pity to think of walking on them.

"Quite marvelous!" judged the Pole, raising a neatly trimmed eyebrow as he scrutinized the final product. "But now you've ruined me! I can't possibly go to my meetings with shoes like these! The soles are too good! See how they shame the shoes!"

"A shoe is what people see," replied Meir, nonchalantly brushing the scraps from his cart, "but the sole is what holds it together. Why shouldn't it receive some special attention from time to time. It's only upon our faith in it that we move from place to place."

"Just what I need; sophistry from a shoemaker. I

have to think of appearances! And these soles make the rest of the shoes look shoddy! I'll double my last offer if you can make the shoes worthier."

Thirty-two rubles seemed like an awesome sum to Meir. He had never seen that much money. Taking back the shoes, he employed his most precious soaps and oils and went over the footwear bit by bit. The minutest details did not escape him. He went so far as to use his thumbnail to push a tiny piece of cloth along the difficult to reach folds and creases where leather met leather. With generous applications of polish and his softest brushes, he buffed a shine up to a radiant glow. On the inside of the shoes, Meir rubbed a fragrant, rose-scented oil.

The merchant pulled back when Meir tried to hand him the shoes. He seemed to be afraid to touch them for fear that they might shatter. Instead, folding his hands on his stomach, he leaned over nervously to peruse them from a distance.

"They are magnificent!" the Pole exclaimed. "Fit for the Czar!"

"Thank you."

"But..."

"But?"

"The laces!"

"The laces?"

"Look how ragged they seem now. They'll never

do. Even if they were new, they'd be no good for shoes like these. Too ordinary. It would jar my associates. They'd lose confidence in me. I could be ruined! I'm going to beat your brains out!"

"Wait! I can make laces!"

"Really? Wonderful! Five rubles for laces fit to tie these shoes! Five more if you don't make me wait until I'm as old as you!"

"Don't move; I'll be right back."

Running as fast as his old legs would go, Meir went home, flew into the house, and began ransacking drawers for something he could make into exceptional laces.

"What am I doing?" he muttered to himself while he searched. "Where am I going to find such fancy laces? Forty-two rubles! Ten just for laces! Anything in this drawer? No! This one? That one over there? Under the bed? Forty-two rubles! The man must be out of his mind! There must be something somewhere! Think! That fop! What does he want, gold?"

At this last thought, Meir heard a click go off in his head. He stopped and waited, listening for his brain to find what it was searching for.

"Gold!" he shouted at last. "Gold! Gold!"

Rushing back into the bedroom, Meir reached for a box on the dresser and removed a small pouch from it. Out of the pouch, he extracted a dusty yarmulke of white satin, profusely decorated with gold stitching. It was the very same cap that he had once bought for the Besht. He had saved it all these years. Holding it up to the sunlight that streamed in through a window, the shoemaker admired how the golden thread still glittered.

With the point of a needle, Meir painstakingly separated the stitching from the satin, taking care not to break it. Perspiring heavily, he cursed his fat hands many times. But when he succeeded in freeing the thread, and was satisfied that there was enough of it for his purpose, he congratulated himself on his ingenuity. Then, folding the fine cord twice over itself, twirling it into twine, cutting it in half and tying the ends, Meir turned it into a superb and perfectly matched pair of laces. Excitedly, he kissed his fingers.

The merchant, tapping his foot impatiently, was still waiting when the puffing shoemaker returned.

"It's about time! I'm missing appointments that I haven't even made yet! I doubt if I have enough time left to beat you properly!"

"Sit," said Meir, and the Pole did. Tugging his shirtsleeves back, the shoemaker kneeled to guide the fellow's feet into the shining red shoes, and then bound them with the golden laces.

"Unbelievable! Breathtaking! Stupendous!" the merchant cheered. "Now, how much was it that I promised you?"

"Forty-two rubles, sir, in all," said Meir, standing proudly at attention.

"Forty-two? For a pair of shoes? Come, I'll grant that you do fine work, but please! We'll split the difference; twenty-one rubles. That is, minus my four ruble commission for finding you the work."

"Commission?"

"That makes seventeen rubles, and it pangs me to pay it. I'm rarely so generous. But you look like a deserving fellow. I'd hate to give you a beating after all this."

Meir's heart sank, though not too far. Seventeen rubles was still a good deal of money. A man could do many things with an amount like that, get a start on something. He had always wanted to build something more than shoes with his hands. Now that he was getting on in years, time was no longer a friend; its current raged against him. This might be his last chance. If he leaned his nose out far enough, his feet would have to follow. The rest was a question of balance. Besides, Meir did not want a beating.

"Seventeen rubles will be fine," he said.

"You drive a hard bargain," the merchant chuckled. "It must be in your Jew's blood to rob us."

Receiving the money, the shoemaker bowed. The Pole nodded in return and went his way. However, after just a few steps, his left foot began to trouble him.

"There must be a pebble in this shoe," he said, looking around for the shoemaker who had already departed.

Leaning against a tree, the merchant slipped off the shoe and shook it. Nothing fell out. He felt around the inside of it; still nothing. The insole was soft, delightfully smooth. It smelled of roses. So, putting the shoe back on, the Pole started off again. A moment later, he felt the same discomfort. Only this time the pebble was in his right shoe. There was nothing for him to do but stop and have another look.

The ritual repeated itself many times; the merchant propping himself up, first on one leg and then the other, as he pulled at the sides of the shoes, peering into them to search out the troublesome rock that leapt mysteriously from foot to foot and always escaped detection. Trying to dislodge the ghostly thing, he slammed the shoes on the side of a building while passersby watched and pointed at him. A group of schoolboys imitated his behavior, removing their own shoes and smacking them against anything that was around.

All of the Pole's efforts failed. He had to walk on the outside edges of the faulty footwear to save his hurt insteps. The rock kept cropping up beneath whichever part of his feet he placed his weight upon as he stumbled along, the boys trailing behind him in kind. Tormented and frustrated beyond endurance, he turned on the brats and threatened to pinch the flesh from their arms if he caught them. The chase ended quickly. The children scattered, leaving the merchant standing back where he had started, in front of Dov Leibish's tannery. Plucking the horrible shoes from his feet, he spat on them and dropped them into a rusty bucket.

"Ouch!" cried a voice from inside the pail.

The bucket shook and jumped and rolled around the merchant on its lower rim, spewing red butterflies with golden markings out of its mouth. The insects were everywhere. Using both of his hands, the Pole barely kept them out of his face enough to breathe. Then he saw something that almost made him swallow his tongue. On one of the butterflies, a tiny figure sat with teeny-weeny legs wrapped around the bug just below its antennae.

"Ahwooo, ahwooo," called the little rider, fluttering into the trees as the merchant's mouth opened in wonder and a score of butterflies flew down his throat.

Meir, unaware of his customer's difficulties, rolled his cart at an easy pace, enjoying the warm day. He walked slowly because his legs were somewhat cramped from all of the running that he had done earlier. Taking a hunk of cheese out of his tool-bag, he carved himself a piece from a corner and popped it into his mouth. He felt fine. The jingle of the money in his pockets was like music, a rhythmically stimulating tune that entered through his ears and carried his thoughts away.

12 🐚

RACHEL WAS IN HER KITCHEN, PREPARING THE afternoon meal for herself and Ezer, when she was distracted by shouts and raucous laughter from outside. Leaning out of the window, she saw that many of her neighbors were rushing down the street. It looked like a celebration; men slapping one another on the back, women buzzing and barely able to contain their own shameless grins as they watched over the children who were skipping and twirling in small, self-contained rings that they made with their hands and used to pull each other along.

"What's the big event?" called Rachel.

"It's Meir!" answered Shmulik the haberdasher. "He's building a shoe for God!"

"Not a shoe," corrected Shmulik's wife, "a boat. I heard, a boat."

"A boat, a shoe, who cares?" countered Shmulik, hurrying his wife along.

The whole neighborhood was gripped by an excitement of anticipation at the shoemaker's mysterious undertaking. Rachel couldn't resist it herself and, tossing her apron behind her, the old woman went off to join in the fun.

"Where do you think you're going?" demanded Ezer, waving his butcher's knife at Rachel as she passed the slaughterhouse. "I haven't eaten!"

She pretended not to hear him.

By the time the butcher's wife arrived at Meir's yard, a crowd had already gathered. It was all that she could do to make out the shoemaker through the moving spaces between the bodies of those who surrounded him. But he was there, sitting under the Mottle-Glückel tree amid piles of planks, boards, and tools, whistling and banging away with a hammer, pausing occasionally to take in the drawing that he had hung from one of the tree's branches.

"Hey Shoemaker, what's up?" teased Yasha the milkman, one hand over his mouth to cover his horsey smirk, nodding to everyone as he awaited an answer.

"I'm making a boat," said Meir. "Don't ask me why. I just feel like making a boat."

"It doesn't look like a boat," continued Yasha, directing everybody's attention to the drawing.

"It's a boat," said Meir.

"It looks like a shoe to me," added Gonif-Yankle the moneylender with a wink to his son, Yitzik-Tushele.

"It's a shoe too," said Meir wearily.

"He thinks he's Noah!" bellowed Ezer as he pushed his way through the throng, wiping his bloody hands on his trousers. "Or maybe he's going to sail us all to Jerusalem for Passover! Has anyone seen my wife?"

"You shouldn't say such things," Rabbi Yacov scolded. "God could hear you and, losing you in a crowd like this, strike one of us by mistake. Be nice, everybody!"

"Sail?" queried Tsoidle the seamstress. "But the river's too far away."

"That's why it's a shoe," explained Yitzik-Tushele. "He's going to have it walk itself to the river."

"That's right," said Meir. "You're a lamp of wisdom. Now, go away."

Pausing from his hammering, the shoemaker pushed people back from his drawing so that he could study it more closely and concentrate on the areas of particular complexity.

"This isn't going to be easy," he mumbled, rubbing the sweat out of the wrinkles on his forehead with his knuckles. Rabbi Yacov was the first to leave. The rest of the neighbors stayed on for some time, mocking the shoemaker's labors with all of the clever sarcasms that they could think up. Only when they ran out of things to say, and grew tired of repeating themselves, did they begin to depart in groups of two and three at a time. Those who had packed picnic lunches left their litter for Meir and the squirrels to worry about. Some others, having slipped nails and wood under their clothing, waved good-bye innocently as they retreated.

For awhile after everyone else had gone, the butcher's wife remained behind, lingering at the edge of the yard. She was terribly curious about Meir's odd behavior.

"Either he never grew up, or he's plain too old," she told herself. "Still inventing things. What does he think he's inventing now?"

Rachel stared and stared until Ezer came up behind her, grabbed her by the bottom, and began to push her home.

The seventeen rubles that Meir got from the merchant didn't last long. After the initial investment in tools and timber, the remaining coins were quickly eaten up by the progress of the work. Although he would have liked to spend all his time on the ship's construction, the shoemaker found that he had to run about like a young man, lining up customers for his shoes so that he could earn money for more supplies. He nearly killed himself. Luckily, Meir's situation changed. He was becoming famous. From towns and villages for miles around, folks came to see the bizarre shoe-boat that was being erected in Warsaw and the addle-brained old man who was responsible for it. Hearing of the legendary eccentricities of Meir's shoes, these visitors purchased them as souvenirs and followed the local custom of giving them away to others. A judge in Zbarazh received a pair from his sister that only walked in the direction that the wind happened to be blowing in. A Polish schoolteacher found a pair on her desk which, when she tried them on, spun her around so forcibly that her dress billowed out, revealing exotically cut undergarments that exposed her tummy, a perfect target for the peashooters of her exuberant pupils. Yet another pair of shoes, discarded in Lublin, found their way into the hands of a couple of aged vagrants.

"These shoes present us with a serious problem, my dear Shmeckele," said the first vagrant.

"Indubitably, my good Peckele," replied the other.

"As I see it; two shoes and..."

"Four feet. Mathematics!"

"Precisely. But there is also an ethical dimension."

"First things first, and the rest will come after of its own accord."

"A pretty point, prettily put, and well-received."

"So, as we've understood, there are two shoes and four feet, algebraically speaking."

"For argument's sake, I concur."

"Therefore each shoe must be filled twice and simultaneously."

"Might I suggest that we, for the sake of simplicity, avoid metaphysics."

"I doubt that we can avoid it, but perhaps we may ignore it. A one-sided division of two performed on the equation and..."

"Two shoes for two feet! We're making progress!"

"But that leaves two extra feet. Which do we keep, and which do we dispose of?"

"My mother always told me that, whenever I am faced with a difficulty, I should put my best foot forward."

"And so you should. A mother doesn't pull her words from trees. She had to learn them from her own mother, and so on back to the ancient days when prophesying was common in the world. My mother also knew something about feet. She wouldn't let me step out of the house unless I put my right foot first. Which, if you'll pardon my asking, is *your* best foot?"

"I, my fine Shmeckele, always leaned toward the left."

"God is smiling on us!"

With deep bows of respect to one another, each of the vagrants took possession of the shoe proper to him; Shmeckele slipping his right foot into the right shoe, and Peckele doing the same with the left. The footwear promptly started to drill into the earth, dragging the vagrants down along a zig-zagging route. When Peckele and Shmeckele finally managed to liberate themselves from the shoes, they poked their heads up in a field where a farmer, following his grandfather's advice on the hunting of gophers, bashed them with a shovel.

All the while, with one thing or another from this quarter and that, Meir was making out quite well. His shoes were selling like noisemakers on Purim. He only wished that the sightseers would go straight home after making their purchases. They were getting to be a nuisance the way they flocked in and out all the time.

Ezer, especially, made it a point to stop by every day to harass the shoemaker. Whichever plank Meir needed at a given moment, the butcher was sure to be standing on it. More often than not, Ezer's foot would beat Meir's hand to the pile of nails that the shoemaker was reaching for and, with a short kick, send the tiny pegs into the weeds. Ezer even gave Meir a new name, which other people soon took up: not "Meir the ship-maker," as Meir thought of himself, but "Meir the noodle-head." Meir wasn't bothered much. He didn't think it was personal. People simply like to have a noodle-head about.

Although the shoemaker wasn't aware of it, he had one other visitor who was as loyal as the butcher. At night, when Ezer was asleep, Rachel tiptoed away and secreted herself behind a corner of Meir's house from where she could view the devoted builder without being spotted herself. In all of her life, she had never seen such a singular sight as Meir at his work, humming to himself, sawing and hammering with no light but that of a small fire. It seemed so utterly senseless and yet, at the same time, so strangely compelling that she could not stay away.

Meir built more determinedly with every passing season. After the first few months, most people lost interest in his doings. They forgot about him. Meir didn't mind. The solitude made it easier for him to concentrate on his work, and the wealth that he had acquired during his popularity was enough for him to see his project through.

Reports of the shoemaker's monumental endeavor were delivered to the magistrate, Wizlo Glemp, on his deathbed.

"I've got them!" strained the dying man, lifting a fist. "I've got those hook-nosed onion-eaters!"

Glemp did not like Jews. At one hundred and twenty-seven, he had long been their most vehement enemy in Warsaw. Stasu, the magistrate's son, had run away with a Jewess. As the elder Glemp saw it, the woman, Yetta, had used obscene and malevolent powers to seduce the boy. She was in league with The Evil One. All Jews were. Didn't they need Christian blood to survive, baking it as they did into their matzohs? Wasn't it a known fact that, dissatisfied with having crucified Christ, they went about stealing the host from churches so as to stab his transubstantiated flesh until blood spurted high enough for them to lap it from the air with their tongues?

For three years, Glemp hunted the couple without success, returning to Warsaw consumed by a desire for vengeance on Yetta's vile race. Fortunately for the Jews, the magistrate could not do much to hurt them. He didn't have the authority, and the Jewish stain in his family made it unlikely that he would ever be appointed to a higher post. An occasional nuisance tax, a payoff to a robber here, an arsonist there, was about all he could muster. So he waited, certain that the devilish Jews would bury themselves in time by committing just the effrontery that he needed to instigate against them effectively. And now, with the news of Meir's boat, his prayers were answered. The sudden delight finished him. But not before he had penned a letter to the governor.

While the magistrate's letter was snaking its way through the corridors and antechambers of the governor's palace, Meir, one year and four months after he had started building, finished his boat. It stood as tall as a house and had the shape of a good, sturdy work boot, except that the sole came down from its sides at steep, inward-pointing angles to form the "V" of the hull. The structure sat on a platform of tree trunks, snugly wedged into carved sections of the logs so that it could remain upright. Meir was pleased with the symmetry of the ship, proud of the strength and straightness of its keel. Climbing a rope ladder, he walked the roofed deck from bow to stern, bouncing a bit to test the supports. He was sure it was seaworthy.

Rubbing his knuckles into the small of his sore back, Meir gave his legs a stretch before he lowered himself to the deck where he lay back with his hands clasped behind his neck. There was a faint, early moon that seemed to balance on the tip of his nose as he watched it. He imagined that he could read his own name in the lines and shadows of its surface.

Late that night, the governor's men went from home to home in the Jewish quarter, rousing the inhabitants and herding them onto the street with shouts and punches. A mounted officer awaited the frightened Jews. Erect and tall, the officer sat with both hands on the reins of his animal, looking out above the heads of his prisoners. Not a hair of the white-blonde curls that stuck out from under his plumed helmet stirred until everyone was quiet. Then, pulling a document from his waistcoat, he began to read.

"Seeing as the Jews have found it fit to create a navy without prior submission of appropriate application, and therefore without the subsequent and necessary approval of proper authorities for such an undertaking, the governor hereby declares the existence of said navy to be unlawful, contrary to the status of Jews as Jews, and detrimental to the security of our beloved Poland and Mother Russia..."

"What navy?" several of the Jews began to whisper at once.

"I don't know about any navy," hissed Gonif-Yankle, eyeing his neighbors.

"It is ordered," continued the officer, "that the aforementioned navy be immediately dismantled and that the following taxes be levied upon the Jewish population of the city, complete payment of same to be made one week from today on pain of expulsion."

"Expulsion?" cried Shmulik the haberdasher. "We don't have any navies!"

"Wood tax, two hundred rubles; nail tax, fifty rubles..."

"It's that shoemaker!" shouted Ezer. "That boat of his!"

"Fees and taxes for mooring an unlicensed vessel within the perimeter of the city, five hundred rubles..."

"Who's going to pay for all this?" demanded Yitzik-Tushele.

"The shoemaker, that's who!" declared Yasha the milkman to the acclamation of most of the others.

"We'll squeeze it from his beard!" pronounced Ezer.

"Haste is a bitter soup," warned Rabbi Yacov, "It satisfieth hunger but maketh cramps."

"Sail tax, fifty rubles; rope tax, twenty-five rubles; fine for building in an undesignated area, four hundred and seventy-five rubles..."

"I'll smash that shoemaker's face!" roared Ezer.

Overwhelmingly, the Jews supported the butcher. Many offered to hold Meir down for him. However, they couldn't make a move until the officer was done with them. Rachel, taking advantage of the confusion that arose while the guards were silencing her neighbors, slipped away. Dressed only in her nightclothes, the old woman hobbled along on her crippled hip to warn Meir of the danger that he was in.

At the shoemaker's house, Rachel shivered in her flimsy bed-gown and pounded on the door. There was no answer. She rattled the hinges with her kicks, and still no answer. Then, hoping either to find Meir at work or a stick to smash a window with, the butcher's wife hurried to the yard where she was stopped breathless at the sight of the shoe-boat.

Meir had neglected to douse his fire, and the way the amber flames reflected on the whitewashed hull of the boat made it vibrate with a shimmering light. Patched cloth, old shirts, and torn trousers had been sewn together into a mighty sail that hung, fore and aft, from the high rigging and flapped in the breezes blowing in from the Vistula. In carefully inscribed, bright orange letters, "The Golden Laces" flickered on the stern. Rachel could hardly believe that she had ever seen the ship before, and that she had watched it take shape day by day. It was magnificent, as if all the beauty that the world promised and sometimes lacked had been nailed into the timbers and stitched into the motley sail.

While Rachel stood, taking in the vision of Meir's vessel, the rest of the community had already been released by the governor's men and were making their way to the shoemaker's home, spitting and growling as they marched. Their own calls for vengeance kept them fired. Yasha and Yitzik-Tushele led the pack with lighted torches. Gonif-Yankle picked up stones and passed them around to eager hands. Ezer, for his part, called threats at the shoemaker that were louder than anyone else's, but fell further and further back until the mob was well ahead of him. At his first opportunity, he slyly removed himself onto a side street.

Ezer laughed. Knowing that there wasn't enough money in the Jewish quarter to pay half of the required taxes, he had come up with a scheme that would turn his neighbors' ill fortune into his own good luck. Weren't there some objects of value in the now vacant homes of his fellow Jews? Weren't there barnloads of oxen and wagons for the taking? Wasn't there a world outside of Warsaw that he and his booty could be in before trouble had a chance to catch up?

Ezer was pushing in doors by the time the noises of the mob reached Rachel and reawoke her to her task. From where she was, she could see Meir where he was stretched out on the deck, sleeping soundly. He didn't respond to her calls, so she took hold of the rope ladder that was suspended along the heel-shaped bow, pulled herself aboard, and hauled the ladder in after her just in time. The angry crowd was in the yard, surrounding the ship. A dozen men clambered onto the ends of the tree trunks that stuck out from under the boat and, with their shoulders to the hull, heaved in an effort to tip it over. Rachel rushed to wake the shoemaker, but the violent rocking of the ship had already done so and he was sitting up, rubbing his eyes. For a moment, the shoemaker didn't know where he was. Seeing Rachel in front of him, he smiled drowsily.

"This isn't a dream!" yelled the old woman. "You're under attack!"

"Burn it!" hollered Gonif-Yankle.

Torches arced through the air and landed at several places on the deck, shooting out sparks on impact. There wasn't time to think. In an instant, Meir was on his feet, squaring the sail so that it billowed with wind. The ship lurched forward. Ropes that held the platform of tree trunks together grew taut and, one by one they snapped, loosing the logs. Rachel ran about the flames, throwing the torches over the side while Meir took the helm of the rumbling boat.

"I've made the damn thing too high!" cried the shoemaker, finding that he had to look between the spokes of the wheel to see ahead, and keep his nose back so that it wasn't struck by one of them as he steered.

The ship pitched dangerously on the logs that were crashing into and turning over one another.

Those who had climbed up on them, now blinded in a spray of splinters, hurled themselves to safety. A number of logs bunched up and lodged into a single, gyrating mass that swelled in front of the boat. Meir gripped the wheel, fractured as it was by the trouncing the ship was taking, and spun it starboard with all of his might, accidentally lobbing off the tip of his nose with a broken spoke in an attempt to avoid catching the great, wooden surge head on. There was a resounding crack. The rudder had split and the blazing vessel, propelled by the force of its own weight, climbed the steep incline of the swell and hurtled out beyond the top of it. When the ship came down, sole first, flat on the head of Yasha the milkman, it shattered into a thousand fiery shards.

Everything was quiet for awhile after the crash. Here and there, bits of timber burned and smoldered. Then people started to move again, moaning, calling for help. Rachel crawled out from under the rubble. When she found Meir, he was perfectly still and his face was covered with blood. Looking at him, her throat tightened. The old woman's heart felt as heavy as brass as she cleaned the blood away with her hands. It was the closest that she had come to the shoemaker since the day that Ezer danced into Praga forest.

The sheer garment that Rachel had been wearing

was gone, lost in the wreck of "The Golden Laces." But when Meir's eyes opened, just a little at first and then as wide as they could be, she was too happy to notice anything else.

13 🙦

EZER COULDN'T STOP LAUGHING. EVERYTHING had gone very well. Having filled several wagons with all sorts of plunder from his neighbors' homes, he was a good distance from the city by the time that ribbons of smoke were rising over the vicinity of the shoe-maker's house. When the smoke cleared, leaving the blue-grey sky clean and clear, he laughed all the harder.

"I'm a sheik!" he proclaimed to the oxen, pricking them with his prod to drive them faster. "Looks like we're the only ones with any brains."

The beasts, frightened by the prodding and the booming voice of the drover, lowed in a dreadful manner. Some stopped in their tracks; others snorted and shook their heads, furiously fighting their halters.

"Get on there!" commanded Ezer, yanking the stationary animals by their snouts. "Back in line!" he hollered, banging the rebellious ones on their heads with his fists.

The oxen got more upset. A wagon turned over. Another followed. A third went into a ditch. Running among the beasts, the butcher battled for order. Harder and harder, he slugged at the oxen's skulls, and they began to fall dead to either side of him. At last, two of the animals broke their bonds and bolted, each trailing a rope that tangled around a separate one of the butcher's ankles. Ezer was cursing and swinging the prod over his head when his feet were snatched from under him. The oxen dragged him for fifteen minutes. Then their paths diverged.

The torn remains of the butcher were discovered a week later by the former inhabitants of Warsaw's Jewish quarter who, after being expelled from the city, had camped nearby. None of the Jews felt very well. Most were bandaged, nursing wounds and cracked bones that were left over from the shoe-boat catastrophe. Finding the goods that Ezer had stolen from them didn't cheer them. Hardly anything was salvageable except for some bits of broken furniture that could be used for firewood and scraps of clothing, furs, and rugs that might be made into blankets. At least many of the oxen were still alive. They would come in handy.

"Praise to the Lord," said Rabbi Yacov, "for taking our animals so that we could find them and be content."

The Jews murmured. They weren't in the mood for praising the Lord. They were worn out. In fact, they had only been able to come as far as they had because Meir had broken open his stock of shoes to provide them all with new footwear for the journey. The shoemaker had worked hard and quickly to fill in the odd sizes in time for the expulsion. But he did a good job. The shoes worked well, so well that the Jews would have kept walking if it weren't that the Sabbath was about to arrive.

"I say we head for Palestine when the Sabbath is over," suggested Dov Leibish.

"Palestine?" responded Pulke, the tanner's wife. "Why not the moon?"

"America!" called Gonif-Yankle. "America! America!"

"Why go anywhere?" asked Meir, leaning toward Rachel as she adjusted the thimble that she had secured to the stump of the shoemaker's nose with a length of string that went over his ears and was tied behind his head. "What's the matter with right here? The ground isn't more solid in other places; the clouds aren't any farther away."

"You can shut up!" snapped Yitzik-Tushele. "It's your fault that we have to go anywhere!"

"America! America!" continued Gonif-Yankle.

"Enough!" insisted the rabbi. "As my predecessor, Rabbi Zaydle, may his memory be blessed in spite of himself, would have said, 'May the next wagging tongue be stiffened with boils!' If your words had no more than an ounce of weight apiece, all creation would be crushed under your stupidity. Palestine? Who made that nice suggestion? What do you think, it's the next village over? And America? With Indians? Lovely. Maybe you think they can fix what's wrong with your heads. And you, Meir, first a shoemaker, then a boat-builder, and now you're a land specialist. What else do you do? Isn't it wonderful that God gave us so many choices that we have to argue about them? We can all go anywhere we like. Wherever I look, I see another direction. But right at this moment the sun is down in each of them. Go clean up for services!"

Though Rabbi Yacov was a champion at making people feel guilty, folks hardly ever obeyed him. This time was no different.

"Why are you all still standing around?" bristled the rabbi.

"I can't move!" cried Tsoidle the seamstress.

"My shoes," moaned Yitzik-Tushele, "they're rooted to the earth. I can't get my feet out of them! That shoemaker—he must have made them with teeth!"

Every Jew was in the same predicament.

"The shoemaker is going to rob us," wept Gonif-Yankle, "and leave us here to die."

"What have you got left to rob?" returned Rachel angrily.

"I did it!" Meir shouted. "I knew I could do it! Shoes that won't walk on the Sabbath! I don't know how, but I did it! I'll paint them all orange for the Besht!"

"All right," said the rabbi. "Everybody calm down. The shoemaker's just having a little joke. Meir, tell your shoes to let us go."

"Tell them? You think they listen to me? I'm as stuck as you are."

The Jews pushed and pulled at their legs, twisting them like the braids of a Challah bread, but Meir's shoes would not give them up.

"Take it easy, everyone," urged the rabbi. "We'll figure this out. God gives tests to make us think. Think! The wise go slow and..."

"Trouble rides a horse!" Dov Leibish cut in, drawing everyone's attention to the sound of galloping horses that were entering the camp.

Twenty of the governor's men had ridden up from the city and were already dismounting. The Jews wanted to run, but the shoes refused. Women clutched their clothing, improvising prayers. Dov Leibish and some of the other men searched the ground for stones.

"Murder! Murder!" shrieked Gonif-Yankle, punching himself in the face.

"What do you want now?" the rabbi demanded of the captain of the guards, the same officer who had read the governor's decree a week earlier.

"All is forgiven," said the officer. "You may return to your homes."

"You mean we can go back to Warsaw and nobody will bother us?"

"You have the word of the governor," replied the officer. "Seems to me that he's decided that having taxpaying Jews around is better than not getting anything. I'm prepared to offer you generous terms of payment on your existing debt, if you'll start packing right away."

The Jews, despite their shouts of acceptance, did not make a move. Looking around nervously, the officer stepped closer to them.

"Didn't you hear me? *Generous* terms."

"We heard you, we heard you," said the rabbi. "It's not so easy."

"Does a twenty percent discount make it easier?"

"Discount?" chirped Gonif-Yankle, dropping to a crouch, wrapping his knees in his arms, and tugging violently.

Again, the officer's words met with eager approval from the Jews who, nonetheless, remained glued to their places, floating embarrassed smiles and squirming in what looked to the officer like a cultic ceremony.

"I don't know what you want," he said, "but don't put any spells on me. I'm just doing my job."

"Spells?" mumbled the rabbi, his attention focused on a stick that he was trying to wedge under the sole of one of his shoes. "No spells, no spells."

Standing back from the Hebrews, the captain hurriedly dispatched a messenger to the city for further orders. Keeping near the horses, he and his men stayed together, eyeing the Jews from a distance. It wasn't until the messenger returned that the captain advanced once more. "I can now promise you a debt reduction of twenty-five percent!"

The chorus of cheers that went up lifted the captain's spirit. Throwing grateful kisses, the Jews blessed his and the governor's names. But not one of them budged an inch.

"Thirty percent!"

"Let us all thank God," spoke the rabbi, "Who, in His wisdom, made ears a part of His creation so that we could hear such good news."

"Amen," responded the congregation. Yet again, not a step was taken.

"Thirty-two percent!"

"Yes! Yes!" chanted the immobile Hebrews.

"Thirty-two and one half percent!"

"Yes!"

Throughout that night and the following day, the captain made proposal after proposal, each one sweeter than the one that came before, while his messenger raced back and forth between the Jewish camp and Warsaw. The Jews bedeviled him. They rejoiced at every turn, but never lifted a foot to reclaim their homes in the city. Then, when the Sabbath was ending and the Jews began to sing songs to it as if it were a young bride who was going off on a journey, the uneasy officer gathered his courage for another effort.

"This is your last chance," he pleaded, restlessly walking among the steadfast Israelites, staring into their faces. "I'm not spending another night out here. Forget the back taxes altogether. Forget the miserable fines. Go to your houses at once and there will be no new taxes for six months. How's that? And every Jew will receive two rubles compensation for the inconvenience of expulsion."

"Two rubles each!" exclaimed Gonif-Yankle as he walked over to a jug of water that stood nearby and dumped its contents out on his head.

"He moved!" shouted Rachel, pointing at the wet moneylender and soon all of the Jews were dancing, jumping, rushing in mad circles as they hugged one another and kissed the shoes that Meir had given them.

"We'll take it!" Rabbi Yacov called to the officer who was hastily climbing his horse to get away from the crazed multitude.

"Get it in writing," whispered Yitzik-Tushele.

The signing took place as soon as everyone could be quieted down, the officer drawing up the paper from atop his horse, handing it to the rabbi to read, and each of them placing his own signature on it in turn. That done, the Jews prepared for the return home.

"Hurry up," said the rabbi, spotting Meir and Rachel standing off to one side. The old couple hadn't done a thing to get ready. "You don't want to be left behind."

"We're not going," said Meir.

"Don't ask us why," added Rachel. "We just don't feel like it."

"Why? We got a good deal."

"A man gets up in the morning and he's breathing; it's a good deal," said Meir.

"This is ridiculous! There's nothing here! Stop trying to sound so mysterious. Come back to the city and the whole neighborhood will help you rebuild your boat."

"No," said Meir, his eyes wandering over the wide

expanse of short, green grass, lingering on the tall poplars and draped willows whose leaves gleamed near the tops where the moonlight was strongest. "I don't think so. We'll stay here and leave when we want to. Maybe we'll go to Warsaw in the morning."

"And maybe not," Rachel put in.

"What about your boat?" asked the rabbi.

"Who needs it?" the shoemaker replied.

"Rachel, have some sense even if he doesn't. What will you do out here? You can't as much as walk straight with your hip."

"I'll do the same as I would anywhere else; limp, one step at a time."

"So all right. What can I do? Listening to you two is giving me a heartburn. That's that and I hope it's good," said the rabbi, taking the thimble-nosed old man and the butcher's widow by the hands and, under a canopy of rags that was held up by whoever could be recruited, married them on the spot.

The Jews of Warsaw mixed congratulations with good-byes and started for home, leaving behind an ox and one of the least damaged wagons for the use of the newlyweds.

"So, old woman," said Meir when he and Rachel were alone, "where would you like to go?"

"We could go looking for a new nose for you," she smiled, snuggling into the shoemaker's arms, her head nestled beneath his chin.

"One is as good as another. They all point somewhere. All you have to do is lean out far enough and..."

"Shhhh," replied Rachel, taking hold of Meir's ears. His thimble was cool as it touched the side of her own nose, but his mouth was very warm.

Photo by Jan Ostan

MARK ARI, a Brooklyn native, is a first generation American whose ancestors included poets, painters, magicians, horse doctors and banjo players. In addition to writing fiction, poetry and articles, Ari works as a musician and artist. His paintings have been exhibited in solo and group shows in New York, Spain and France, and he has presented original performance pieces in a number of American cities. He teaches writing at Brooklyn College of the City University of New York.

The Shoemaker's Tale *was
designed using PageMaker version 4.2,
set in 13 point Adobe Janson and output on a
LaserMaster 1000 plain paper typesetter at
Type for U, Cambridge, Massachusetts.*

*Printed by Cushing-Malloy, Inc.,
Ann Arbor, Michigan.*

∽